Oath of Allegiance

AN ALLISON QUINN THRILLER

BOOK FOUR

VANNETTA CHAPMAN

OATH OF ALLEGIANCE

Requests for information should be addressed to: VannettaChapman (at) gmail (dot) com

Cover design: Streetlight Graphics

First printing, 2025

ASIN: B0DSCL6DYG

in loving memory of
Steve Van Riper

“I, Allison Quinn, do solemnly swear
that I will support and defend
the Constitution of the United States
against all enemies, foreign and domestic;
that I will bear true faith and allegiance to the same;
that I take this obligation freely,
without any mental reservation or purpose of evasion;
and that I will well and faithfully discharge
the duties of the office on which I am about to enter.
So help me God.”

"Many that live deserve death.
And some that die deserve life."

~J.R.R. Tolkien

Chapter One

Allison Quinn chose the town of Childress, in the panhandle of the Lone Star State, by closing her eyes and putting a finger on the Texas page of the bound road atlas she held in her lap. Two hours north of Aunt Polly's ranch. Secondary roads. Little chance of being picked up by any electronic monitoring.

Edward Dominguez drove.

Neither of them carried cell phones. Two hundred and twenty-three smart phones had exploded in the last six months, killing all two hundred and twenty-three people holding them, injuring another three hundred and forty-six that were standing close by. Smart watches, fitness trackers, self-driving cars, laptops, routers, pacemakers. If it could be hacked, if it could be turned into a weapon, it had been. Not all of them, of course. Actually, only a small percentage.

But enough to put the American people on edge.

The truck Edward drove was a 1962 model, built before GPS trackers and back-up cameras and onboard computer systems that could be hacked.

Allison had known Edward all of her life. She had exchanged hugs with him exactly three times—the day she'd moved to Aunt

Polly's ranch after her father had been killed, the day she'd graduated from college, and the day she'd come home wounded and in need of a place to heal.

The old vaquero pulled up to an abandoned Texaco station, shoved the gearshift into park, and got out of the truck. By the time Allison had shouldered her pack, he had opened the passenger door, and for the fourth time in her life, she walked into his arms.

"Take care of Polly."

"Take care of yourself." Tears glistened in his eyes that were a brown the color of all things good—chocolate cake and the bark of oak trees and rich, Texas dirt.

He put his weathered hands on her face—hands that felt as soft as the most expensive leather—and looked her in the eyes. "Vaya con Dios."

She nodded, unable to speak.

He resettled his sweat-stained hat on his head, climbed back into the vintage truck, and drove south in the direction they had come.

Childress was not Allison's ultimate destination. She still had many miles to go, and she could have boarded a Greyhound bus that still picked up travelers at the old depot.

She didn't.

Instead, she walked to the edge of town, stuck out her thumb, and within twenty minutes had hitched a ride.

The woman who pulled over to pick her up sported a Remington rifle in a gun rack positioned across the back window. She looked to be in her late fifties or early sixties with red hair beginning to streak gray. The truck was an older model Ford 150, and the load she pulled on a large flatbed was hay. Her face was free of make-up and her gaze direct. She did not look like the type to suffer fools or pick up hitchhikers.

"Where ya headed?"

Allison shrugged.

"Get in."

This woman had apparently seen it before. People headed somewhere else. The particular direction didn't matter.

"Name's Martha. My momma had a thing for Biblical women. God bless her soul."

"Thanks for the ride." Allison didn't offer her name, and Martha let that slide.

As they travelled north on US-62, Martha talked of her three sons. One had served in Iraq. One was currently teaching U.S. History in the Dallas area. A third had died of a drug overdose.

They crossed the Prairie Dog Fork of the Red River, turned east and travelled for an hour without seeing another town. Martha described her husband, Jethro, who had inherited the two-section ranch where their three-bedroom house had been built in 1951. "His parents' house, then ours. Most parts of the country talk about acreage, but here ... in the panhandle ... it's sections. Each section is a square mile or 640 acres. I see you're wondering why I'm telling you this, but it helps if you can picture the thing."

She waved out the window at the landscape. They were passing through the southern portion of the Great Plains—flat terrain, semi-arid climate, dust and grasslands. "Not so different from what you're seeing now. Two sections. One thousand, two hundred and forty acres."

Her voice filled with pride even as she described rising costs and falling profits and the hardscrabble existence of making a living as a rancher. Her husband, Jethro, had passed three years earlier from lung cancer.

"Small cell. I buried him four months after the diagnosis. No fault of the doctor. Jethro was stubborn. Refused to go in for a cough that kept him up at night." She smiled at some tender memory, shook her head, told the rest of it. "Said if he went to the doctor for every little thing, the ranching would never get done. By the time he was coughing up blood and I insisted, the malignant cells had spread to damn near every organ."

"I'm really sorry."

Martha shrugged. "Life is hard. The Good Book tells us as much. Didn't expect it, though. Didn't expect to lose him so soon. We only had forty-two years together and while that might sound like an eternity to someone your age, I assure you it is not enough."

Allison nodded. Thought of Aunt Polly. Thought of her father.

They crossed into Oklahoma and the plains gave way to small mesas and rocky outcroppings.

"I was a smoker, too. Stopped the day Jethro found out about the cancer. We both did. My only vice now is these diet drinks." She reached down into the mid-sized cooler that sat on the floorboard between the two front seats, shook off the ice, and popped the top on the third she'd had in the last ninety minutes. "Might as well get you one. You know you want it."

Allison reached into the cooler and fetched a can, though she didn't want it. The aspartame was too sweet and left a bitter aftertaste. She understood that listening to the stories and drinking the pop was the price for the ride.

Martha had three grandchildren. She spent the last part of their time together describing the children's success in school, the way they excelled in sports, how each and every one seemed to have inherited Jethro's stubbornness.

When they pulled into the outskirts of Lawton, Allison said, "I'll get out here."

If Martha was surprised, she didn't show it.

Instead, she found a safe place to pull over, which was easy to do as there was very little traffic on the road. She reached into the cooler to fetch Allison another can of pop. Took her time wiping off the ice. Looked her directly in the eye when she pushed it into her hands. "What's happening in this country right now—it isn't natural. People shouldn't be at the mercy of machines. You seem to have a good head on your shoulder, but promise me you'll watch out."

Allison nodded and accepted the soda.

Martha wished her safe travels, waved, then pulled back onto the road.

Nearly six hours had passed since Allison had left Aunt Polly's ranch. She carried nothing that had an electronic signal. Carried nothing except the pack. She glanced down at the old Timex watch, then mentally checked off what was in the pack:

- A very good fake ID that she'd purchased from a man in Highland Hills on the south side of San Antonio
- One box of energy bars
- Three bottles of water
- The road atlas
- The Glock that she'd carried since her first day on the job for Homeland Security. Hadn't failed her in twelve years. Wouldn't fail her now.
- Two boxes of extra ammunition
- A medical kit
- Two thousand dollars cash

The pack was old—something Aunt Polly had pulled from a back closet. The water-resistant watch had been her father's—a Timex that had hands instead of a digital read out. Absolutely nothing in her pack or on her body could be tracked, and still her glance darted toward the sky, scanning for drones or the glint of a satellite. Nothing. Nothing she could see or hear, anyways.

The noonday sun beat down on her. She veered from the road when she spied a stand of trees. Walked into the midst of their canopy. Sat with her back against one of the trunks and her hat pulled down low over her eyes. She wouldn't sleep, but she would rest.

The silence was a balm after riding with Martha. Allison drank it in as if it were a needed, tall glass of cold water.

Settled in to wait for dark.

She'd catch the bus then. If the last had passed through, she'd catch the first one in the morning.

She checked her watch once more.

Next stop was Hays, Kansas, where Donovan and Kate were to meet her. Donovan would bring a vehicle. Kate would bring her talents, which far exceeded Allison's. The woman was a tech whiz with an eidetic memory. The best of the best. How else could she have survived two years living under the gaze of John Howard?

Allison opened the road atlas, measured off the distance which looked to be just shy of three hundred and fifty miles. A bus would cover that distance in seven hours, maybe six, depending on the number of stops. She had slightly less than twenty-four hours to get there. One way or another, she'd arrive early, scope the location, make sure neither of her friends had picked up a tail. Donovan wasn't her boss on this particular op. He was the man she loved, and she could trust he would follow her instructions, which she'd sent the old-fashioned way via the United States Postal Service. She didn't doubt Donovan or Kate, but she understood too well the skill and technical expertise of the man hunting her.

John Howard wouldn't hold anything back this time.

The thought of that brought a smile to her lips.

Game on.

Katelyn Ballou reported to Reid Clark's office at exactly eighteen hundred hours. He nodded toward the chair across from his desk, so she sat and waited as he pounded out one last email. Satisfied with what he wrote, he tapped send, pushed the keyboard away and focused his attention completely on her. Clark was her boss. More importantly, he was one of the few people who had known her identity while she was working undercover for John Howard.

Kate Jackson.

She had been Kate Jackson for two years. All of her life, she'd gone by Kate, so the alias had felt natural.

She'd worked in that lair of John's and Stella's for twenty-four months, and when she'd finally fled, she'd been certain he would track her, then kill her. That hadn't happened, though. And now she was here, once again following the directions of Reid Clark.

Or more accurately, of Allison Quinn, who worked for Reid Clark.

Clark had been her lifeline during those long two years, though she hadn't been able to communicate directly with him. Knowing he was there had brought a measure of comfort.

Now he sat back and steepled his fingers.

"Where is she?"

"I'm not sure."

"You're her partner."

She shrugged.

"I assume you have received directions on where to meet her?"

Kate held up a stamped envelope, as yet unopened.

Clark closed his eyes as if to count to ten, but they immediately popped open again.

"You don't know where you're going."

"I don't. My instructions are to meet her at noon tomorrow. The location is in this envelope. Allison insisted I not open the envelope while in this building, or in any building. Her suggestion was to go to a park or a forest and open it."

He crossed his arms and studied her.

When she added nothing, he sighed. "I'm worried about Allison. She didn't pick up the alias ID we created for her."

Kate held his gaze. She'd become quite good at being questioned while she'd been inside Middle-earth, as John Howard had liked to call his operating center. She'd become good at waiting.

"Can I assume she has another?"

"Yes."

"One that isn't agency created?"

"Yes."

"She honestly thinks they've infiltrated our communication system."

"It is a possibility."

"Yeah. It is." He ran a hand over his balding head. "Let me see if I have this right. Allison's gone off the grid—completely. She's depending on her own resources, because she suspects we might have been hacked and/or have an informant in our midst. You're going to meet her, but you don't know where until you open that envelope. And since Donovan put in for a week of personal days..." He put the last two words in air quotes. "I assume he's helping as well."

"Correct."

"And do you really think that John Howard is going to have guessed where you're going?"

"It wouldn't be a guess. He has ways of gathering information."

"Ways that exceed this task force, Homeland Security, and the Agency?"

"At times."

"You think you know where his next attack will take place?"

"We do."

"And it's not on the watch list?"

"It's not."

Clark blew out a breath. "The best our AI program could offer was half a dozen possibilities, and we fed everything into the system that we had on John Howard, Stella Gonzalez, Anarchists for Tomorrow, and all of the information we found in Whitefish, Montana that they left behind."

"If they left it behind, we can assume it was misdirection."

"The program agrees with you."

Reid stared at a point on the far wall. Kate waited.

"Explain to me how you two can, with any degree of confidence, know where he's going to be?"

"Instinct. I worked closely with John and Stella, so there's a solid chance I can predict their next move and the one after that. This is personal for them. At least, it is for Stella. Her motivation has something to do with the murder of Arthur Quinn."

"We haven't found that connection yet. John Howard we know a lot about. To some extent, we understand what happened and why he went rogue. We know he's former military, know what happened to his family, know when he went off the grid. We can make an educated guess at when he connected with the AT. Stella—we have nothing on her and certainly no connection to Allison or Allison's father." He propped his elbows on the table, rested his forehead in his hands, looked more tired and vulnerable than she'd ever seen him.

"We're going to catch John and Stella," Kate said. "We're going to stop this."

His gaze drifted to the screen on the wall, which displayed a countdown clock.

Current day/time: July 1, 18:14
ETA: July 4, 12:01 a.m.
Time until ETA 2 days, 5 hours,
45 minutes, 54 seconds

Estimated Time of Attack. They didn't actually know when John and Stella would make their move, but the program, Kate, and Allison all agreed it would be on July 4th. That was too big of an opportunity for him to miss. His ego and her psychosis would demand it.

"I don't have to tell you how bad the last fifteen months have been. You've seen the casualty numbers. I also don't have to remind you that major players—on both sides of the political aisle—are on the verge of snapping. This country is ready to fly apart at the next intrusion, the next electronic device that blows up in a friend's hands, the next—" He stopped abruptly. His scowl deepened.

"We believe we are closing in on John Howard's site." He told her the location.

Kate shook her head. "He had no holdings there that I knew of."

"Okay. I'll relay that, but we'll continue to pursue. We also have teams deployed to the top twenty potential sites for the next attack. If you end up at one of those, please coordinate with the lead on the ground. I don't want either of you mistook for a terrorist and shot."

"Will do, boss."

"If I don't know what name you're traveling under, how do I know if you need help?"

"We'll call."

"And if I have to identify your body?" The weariness crept into his eyes. "How do I do that, Kate, if I don't even know..."

Before he could finish, she pulled one more envelope from her shoulder bag and slid it across the desk.

"Our aliases are in there. Allison asked that you not open it until at least forty-eight hours after the event . . . whatever the event happens to be."

He nodded once, stood, shook her hand.

"You're a hell of an agent. All three of you are, but this thing..." He moved around the desk, then walked with her to the closed door. "It's bigger than any of us. Be careful."

Kate grinned in response. She wasn't naive, but she thought, given her technological expertise, Allison's bulldog tenacity, and Donovan's ability to see and appropriately respond to the big picture, that they had a good chance of stopping John Howard, Stella Gonzalez and the Anarchists for Tomorrow. They weren't arrogant, but they were as prepared as they could be. And they were invested. Like Stella Gonzalez, for them, this had become personal.

As her friend liked to say, "Game on."

Chapter Two

Allison couldn't have picked a better location if she'd spent days researching. She hadn't spent days researching, and she hadn't used Google or Wikipedia or any other web program designed to make her life easier.

She'd sat on Aunt Polly's back porch with the same road atlas she now carried in her pack and used an old compass with a number 2 pencil that was in her dad's box of things. What had he used it for? The same thing she was doing? Had he worried about being followed? Even then? Even in 1996, before wireless connections and smart phones and social media?

Allison had put the point of the compass on Mount Rushmore, stretched out the compass to what seemed a safe enough distance, and drawn a circle. That circle had gone directly through Hayes, Kansas. She'd written the location in two envelopes along with the date and time, then mailed one to Donovan and the other to Kate.

She'd guessed there would be a golf course—there was.

And she'd suspected no one would be on playing the ninth hole in the sweltering heat at high noon—correct again.

She watched Donovan park the old model Ford Bronco at the

edge of the lot. The vehicle had obviously seen better days. Perfect.

He sauntered toward the ninth hole, stopping now and then to pick up golf balls. Donovan looked good. Better than he had two months ago when they'd spent a weekend together in Monte Vista, Colorado. Better than she remembered.

The ninth hole wasn't far off the concrete path that meandered through the course. There were even a few tall shrubs to afford them a small degree of privacy should anyone be watching. From her vantage point, she'd also be able to see anyone approaching. Or so she thought, until Kate popped out of a rather small stand of trees, sporting a backpack and carrying two black bags. How long had she been in there? Allison didn't bother to ask. The woman had skills. Five foot ten, thin, twenty-eight years old, beautiful.

Kate brushed a few leaves out of her shoulder-length, black hair, then moved next to Allison. "He looks healed from that cruise ship fiasco."

"Oh yeah. Donovan's one hundred percent." Allison tried to temper her grin, but she wasn't successful. Kate nudged her shoulder with her own, and Allison felt like they were college girls mooning over a boy.

"What are you two grinning about? It's hot as hell out here."

Donovan was Black, 38 years old, and still retained the physique of the line-backer he had been in college. His hair, as usual, was buzz cut. Only his eyes betrayed the seriousness of their situation.

"Kansas in July, and you're complaining?" Allison put her arms around him, breathed in the smell and steadiness of him, then stepped back.

"Kate."

"Donovan."

He handed Allison the Bronco's keys. "Thank you for not grilling me on whether I followed your directions. I did, even if I think they were a little over the top."

"Only a little?" Allison pocketed the keys.

"For what it's worth, I agree with Allison. John has back doors into all of the facial recognition systems."

"But that's too much data to cull through—"

"Not for John. Or Stella. Not for the Anarchists. They have more computer power than the task force."

"That's not possible."

"Not in the old sense, but systems are smaller now. Mobile. John and Stella will spend whatever it takes. The task force has..."

"Limits. Guidelines. Other concerns." Donovan stuck his hands in his pockets. "I'm aware. So where to from here?"

"Mount Rushmore," Allison said.

"Rushmore. As in South Dakota?"

"The same."

Kate added, "We'll take secondary roads all the way."

"Shouldn't be a problem as far as surveillance between Kansas and South Dakota. I'm not sure people in these rural towns have heard of traffic cameras."

"Oh, they've heard of them." Allison continued to scan the golf course. "They just said a polite *no thanks* to being tracked."

The three of them had backed up, so that they were standing in the shade of the cluster of trees Kate had popped out of.

"You both should know that we don't have an agency team at Mount Rushmore," Donovan said. "The program picked the top twenty potential sites, but South Dakota wasn't one of them."

"Understood," Allison said.

"We'll be fine," Kate added.

"Uh-huh. All the same, I'd like to re-direct one of our teams."

"No!" Both women shouted the word at once, then glanced at each other and shrugged.

Donovan threw his hands in the air, palms out. "Thought you might say that. I'll meet you in Custer then."

"Not going to happen." Allison emphatically shook her head. "Donovan, you have to show up at your assigned location or the Anarchists will know..."

"I'm way ahead of you. One of our agents suffered a complicated leg break while trying to skateboard with his teenaged son. He's registered in the hospital under my name, and should anyone show up to check, they'll find a slightly less good-looking black man. Same size. Same stats. They'll see what they expect to see—me."

Allison crossed her arms, trying to think of a reason that what he was proposing wouldn't work, but Kate got there first. "There are cameras all around Mount Rushmore. They'll pick you up."

"We both know they'll pick the two of you up, too. At that point, whatever happens, happens. If it seems prudent leading up to the Estimated Time of Attack, I'll remain at base camp. We have three rooms at the lodge in the state park, all reserved under our aliases."

Allison realized there was no arguing with him. She also understood she felt better with him there. He'd be a valuable addition to the team. "Okay. But we travel separately."

"You're not going to let me drive the Bronco?"

"You drove it here."

"How am I supposed to get to Custer?" He was grinning as he said it.

"You already have a way to Custer because you knew I'd insist that we drive separately."

Kate held out her hands for the SUV's keys. "I'm going to store my gear while you two work out the details." She walked away with a smile and a wink.

"Kate's an excellent partner for you," Donovan said.

"You're an excellent partner for me."

"Agreed." He pulled her into the circle of his arms, held her as if it might be the last time.

She felt it too—this teetering on the edge of a terrible storm. "Together, the three of us should be able to take down one megalomaniac."

"Did you tell her about the messages you received?"

"Not yet."

"Don't leave her in the dark."

"I won't."

Donovan kissed her on the top of the head, and when he did, Allison realized how tired she was. The terrorist attack on the cruise ship that had injured Donovan had happened fifteen months earlier, and they had endured one attack after another since. Some of those the public knew about, but not all.

She'd visited Donovan in the hospital once. They'd had two weekends together, worked as part of a larger team on half a dozen ops, and shared exactly eight private meals.

As if he could read her mind, he said, "We're going to Aunt Polly's after this."

She pulled back from his embrace to look at him. His tone had dropped. His smile became more tender.

"Seriously?"

"Yeah." He ran a thumb along her jaw line. "Why are you surprised?"

"Didn't know you were into small town Texas vacations."

"Who said it would be a vacation?"

She felt her eyebrows shoot up.

"You don't think about quitting?"

"I think about it."

"But—"

Allison shook her head. Quitting wasn't seriously on her radar at this point. What was happening in America was a tragedy. And what she feared would happen in less than two days would be worse. It would be devastating to the country and a personal affront to her. John Howard or Stella Gonzalez or both were somehow connected to her father's murder, and she intended to find out how. She would learn the truth, discover if anyone still alive and involved in that crime could be brought to justice, then see that it was done.

Or she would kill them.

Were she to be honest, she preferred the latter to the former.

Sheridan, Wyoming, was significantly larger than Whitefish, Montana.

More people.

More chance of being noticed.

Still, it was a good fallback position, and John Howard had moved his staff there within twenty-four hours of Kate Jackson's betrayal. Since that day, he'd also insisted that all employees agree to GPS implants. The technology was supposedly still in the research stage, mainly because of ethical concerns. John had no such issue with them, and any employee that resisted was let go. Only one chose that route, and that person did not know the location of their new base camp. He could have killed her, but he suspected that she'd squirreled away evidence that would be released when she didn't check in. Jocelyn Green was no one's fool. She hadn't worked for the enemy. She wasn't in collusion with Kate, but she also didn't have the stomach for what they needed to do.

He didn't regret that she left.

He did hate losing one of his best programmers. Still, he liked the paired down look of things—five programmers and a dozen security staff. They would make it work. They had made it work for over a year, and they'd made significant progress.

Stella strode into the control center with the aplomb of a queen deigning to check in on the servants.

"Where are we?" She rattled the ice in her drink.

Honestly, he didn't understand how she could operate on so little food and so much alcohol. It offended his sense of order and discipline. He wouldn't have tolerated it in a subordinate. Unfortunately, Stella Gonzalez was still financing this endeavor.

"Explosives are in place, diversionary operations are proceeding as planned, and we've infiltrated all security systems."

"Do they know we're in their network?"

John nodded toward Spencer, who pushed up his glasses and said with a stifled laugh, "They're not even looking."

"You're certain about that?"

He blinked several times, took off his glasses, polished them, and put them back on before muttering, "Of course I'm certain."

There was something about his tone that Stella didn't like. Although John detested working with her, although he lived for the day when he would be financially independent, sometimes he enjoyed watching the show she put on.

Stella carefully set her vodka and ice down at her station. It wasn't a work area so much as a throne. A small marble table sat in front of the chair. The chair was plush red velvet—almost comical in contrast to the rest of the room. Of course, it pivoted so she could pierce anyone with her glare. Stella was in her mid-seventies. She had a personal vendetta that John had never quite understood. He didn't need to understand. She was useful to him, and that was reason enough to tolerate her presence.

State-of-the-art monitors covered three walls of the control room. The only exit from the room as well as an in-wall drink center adorned the last wall. Kate had been the one to convince him that if he kept a mini fridge stocked with red bull, liquor, and diet drinks, his programmers would work thirty percent longer before crashing.

Stella walked a slow circuit around the room. She was wearing a leotard type dress that would have looked appropriate on a twenty-year-old. Her nails were painted black—long, sleek, possibly lethal. When she reached Spencer's station, she stopped behind his chair and ran one fingernail slowly along the back of his neck.

"Nature hosts many wonderful things, Spencer. Take, for example, batrachotoxin. Have you heard of it?" She leaned forward so that she could offer him a chilling smile, still leaving that single nail on the back of his neck. "Batrachotoxin is an alkaloid toxin found in the golden poison dart frog. A mere two micrograms can kill a person. Imagine if that were to be mixed into fingernail polish."

She cackled, and the sound was more disturbing than any threat she might have whispered in his ear. Spencer's complexion turned a chalky white, and he seemed to hold his breath until Stella tapped his cheek with the same nail, returned to her throne, picked up her drink, and sashayed out of the room.

John wanted to laugh out loud.

He wouldn't put poisoned fingernail polish past her.

Making a mental note to shoot her if she tried to touch him with those nails, he spent another twenty minutes monitoring the South Dakota situation, then returned to his office. Once there, he pulled out his Starlink phone and accessed the encrypted messaging program.

A single notification waited for him. He tapped it.

Delivery of M2 to agreed location by eighteen hundred hours on requested date—confirmed.

As he watched, three little dots appeared, then the words—

Balance of payment due.

He'd had Jasmine working on a side project for the last six months. They'd been slowly bleeding money from the U.S. Treasury, which he found both humorous and ironic. The U.S. government was so far in debt that they'd never notice a few million dollars missing. They'd assume that it was being spent on military black ops. In the meantime, John had accrued the funds that he needed to make his dream a reality.

Which wasn't quite right.

It wasn't his dream to release a plague on America.

However, what he'd attempted to do over the last few years

was not working. The American people weren't waking up. When he exploded their phones, did they give up the damn things? Did they stop staring at them 24 hours a day? They did not. Instead, a tech billionaire mass produced what basically amounted to a pocket-sized faraday cage that retailed at $199 and sold out in less than an hour. When he hacked into their self-driving cars, government officials blamed it on the manufacturer and announced a recall.

Smart watches had received an upgrade that had kept his hackers out.

Fitness trackers and laptops and routers and medical devices that could track a person's every move were all selling at higher rates than before the attacks. How was that possible? How could the American people be so addicted to their devices that no risk seemed too great a risk? That living without them was inconceivable?

He'd given the general populace plenty of chances to see the light, to throw off the oppressive cloak of modern technology and government surveillance. They'd refused at every opportunity. He didn't want to release a military-grade contagion across these United States. He loved his country. But he would not stand idly by and watch it destroy itself.

He typed—

Initiating transaction

Then he accessed his financial app by touching the pad of his index finger to the screen. Once the program confirmed the funds were transferred, he turned off the device.

It was done.

There was no way to stop it now.

Should everyone in his operation, including Stella and himself, be killed in the next hour, his plague would still be released. His pre-recorded message would still be broadcast. He'd rather do it live though. People seemed to enjoy live-streaming.

Things were about to get very messy.

And the American people had no one to blame but themselves.

Chapter Three

They avoided even medium-sized towns. Took state roads instead of the interstate.

Drove west to Oakley, northwest to Colby, then due north to Culbertson. Nebraska was wide-open prairie, and Allison wondered what Martha would say about the view that stretched to the horizon.

What's happening in this country right now, it isn't natural.

She was correct in so many ways. It wasn't natural for there to be seventy thousand people in a square mile, and yet Manhattan existed. It not only existed, it flourished. Fewer and fewer people understood where their food came from. Projections showed that on-line education would quickly outpace in person instruction, even in the public-school sector.

"What are you chewing on over there?" Kate asked. She'd taken over driving when they'd hit the Nebraska state line.

Allison had thought she might sleep, but instead she was wide awake, her thoughts working over the problems of the world, her eyes scanning the horizon as if John Howard might drop from the clear blue sky.

"I was thinking about Martha."

"Martha?"

"Farmer. Texas Panhandle. Gave me a ride."

"Ah."

"She said that people shouldn't be at the mercy of machines."

"Insightful."

"I suppose she's able to understand that because she doesn't need those machines, or she doesn't think she needs them. She was hauling hay from the Texas panhandle to Lawton, Oklahoma. Sixty something years old, widowed, and still working the land."

"My people are from Iowa. It's a different life there. It's hard to imagine the technological horrors we deal with when you're walking across a field of corn that's taller than you are."

"Yeah." Allison leaned her head back against the seat rest. "Yeah, it is."

And then she slept, though her dreams were muddled. Donovan was fishing, but he kept pulling up black boxes. Aunt Polly stood on the porch, hands shading her eyes so that she could better scan the horizon as a tornado tore across her land. Her father telling her to run. She fell into the dream as if it were waiting for her, knowing even as her heart raced and sweat slicked her palms that she was powerless to stop what happened next.

Only nine years old.

Terrified, confused, and utterly helpless.

Her legs shook, and twice she nearly tripped before she stopped and pressed her back against the far side of a towering redwood tree.

Her chest ached as if she'd run much farther than she had. Her breath escaped in quick, short bursts.

She needed to be quiet.

She needed to be still.

Their campsite remained within sight. All she had to do was step around the tree and open her eyes. She didn't. He'd told her to run. He'd meant for her to hide. It kept her from seeing, but it didn't prevent her from hearing.

"You shouldn't have tried to stop me."

The bang, when it came, echoed through the forest, sliced through her soul. Allison squeezed her eyes shut tight, felt the tears slip down her cheeks. She wouldn't look. She'd be as quiet as a mouse. As still as a rabbit.

But her heartbeat was too loud. The man in the ski mask would hear. He'd find her and then—

Sweat dripped down her face. She could feel the roughness of the tree through her clothes. Looking down, she saw she'd torn the fabric of her Dora the Explorer shirt when she'd nearly fallen.

"Run."

"You shouldn't have tried to stop me."

Bang.

The three moments played in a seemingly endless loop.

She waited—shivering, terrified.

She knew he was dead. Knew she would miss him for the rest of her life. She experienced the nightmare as both the child she had been and the woman she now was. She struggled to open her eyes and saw—

She woke with a gasp.

"You okay?" Kate tossed her a worried look.

Allison sat forward, pressed her shaking hands to her face. It was the dream—the same dream-again. But this time, something was different. This time, the killer was....

But she couldn't reach it.

What had she seen?

What had been different?

The images slipped away, gone as surely as the childhood she'd had ripped from her on the day her father was murdered.

"I was thinking we need food," Kate said. "This place look okay to you?"

Allison nodded. Kate pulled over and parked in front of a burger joint with outdoor seating, and suddenly Allison was starved. When had her last meal been? That morning at Aunt Polly's? No, that was the day before.

"Yeah." Alison released her seatbelt. "This'll do. Where are we?"

"Holdrege, Nebraska."

"Small town."

"Population: Five thousand, five hundred, and fifteen."

"Works for me. Also, I'm starved."

Nebraska was an open carry state. As they got out of the Bronco, she spotted one, two, at least three people wearing a holster. It wasn't the wild west, but it wasn't far from it. No security cameras that she could see.

Just a burger place in small town Nebraska.

Still, she pulled her ball cap down lower.

Kate did the same. As they walked toward the order window, Allison noticed signs posted every ten to fifteen feet.

All cellular devices must be in a Quantum-Guard Pouch

Which wasn't a problem for Allison or Kate, since neither was carrying a cell phone.

Allison had been at her Aunt Polly's for the last several weeks. She couldn't remember seeing any such pouches before, though she had gradually become aware that some people were now leaving their cell phones in their cars or mailboxes rather than bring them into their home. She stepped closer to Kate. "Is that normal? Requiring the pouches?"

"More and more."

"Do they work?"

"Who knows? People think they work. I've seen some YouTube videos where they remotely detonate a phone in a QuantumGuard Pouch. The pouch holds. They're made from layered conductive and magnetic materials."

"Basically, an EMP shield."

"Yeah, but less bulky than the first models, and the device can still be used while in the pouch, which is quite advanced."

"Someone's making a billion dollars."

"Maybe more."

Allison placed their order, while Kate grabbed a table on the fringe of the sitting area. She paid, then picked up napkins and drinks which she deposited on their table. Kate sat facing the other customers. Allison faced the fields that fanned out and away from the place. There was still plenty of sunlight. Night time in the summer didn't come to Nebraska until nearly nine p.m.

"How long was I out?"

"An hour, maybe a little longer. You had the nightmare again?"

"I did."

Allison had grabbed a large water for Kate, who drank nothing with sugar, and a can of soda for herself, hoping the caffeine would give her at least a brief surge of energy. The soda was ice cold and the sugar refreshing in a way that surprised her. Completely different from Martha's diet drinks.

Their order number was called, and Allison grabbed the food. They'd worked all these details out weeks ago when they'd first conceived going off on their own. Wherever they stopped, only one person would interact with the public. Hopefully, it would reduce their chances of being noticed, of being on camera, together. That was something John Howard would look for.

Allison bit into the burger and nearly groaned. It was hot off the grill. The cow had probably been raised at a local ranch. For all she knew, the cheese came from a dairy farm in the northeast part of the state. Around her second bite, she said, "I've been getting messages."

"What kind of messages?"

"From John. I think."

Kate put her burger down in the little plastic basket and wiped her fingers on a napkin.

"When did this start?"

"A month ago."

"Why are you just now telling me?"

"I don't know."

Kate waited. Donovan had been right. She was an excellent partner. Allison had the sinking sensation that she shouldn't have held back. If she'd told her earlier, maybe she could have made some sense of it.

"I was afraid you'd pull out."

"That won't happen. I'm not going anywhere."

"I know that now."

Kate picked up her burger, took another bite, chewed, and swallowed. "What did they say?"

"At first they felt kind of random, and I didn't want to google it because..."

"He'd pick up on the digital signature."

"Right."

"If it was him."

"Yeah." Allison reached for a french fry, chose one covered with salt and pepper, dipped it in the ketchup. "The messages came in on my task force phone—another reason I think they've been compromised."

"Or someone who's a little off happens to have your number."

"My Aunt Polly figured it out. Each message was a reference from *Lord of the Rings*. She said my dad loved those books. He would read parts of them to her when they were growing up."

"Okay."

"I found the name Gollum in my dad's papers."

"Huh. So, it's possible there's a connection."

"I think so."

"There were references to Gollum in your field reports from the Grand Canyon op."

"Yeah. And Blitz, one of the operatives at the Grand Canyon, mentioned Frodo. Said my dad was code-named Frodo."

"Wow."

"An associate of my father's, a man who worked for the agency named Edgar Burch, also confirmed that his dark web name was Frodo." Allison pulled a sheet of paper from her pocket, unfolded it, then slid it across the table to Kate.

A hunted man wearies.
Meet revenge with revenge.
Stray. And fail.
The storm comes.
You shall not pass!

Kate tapped the last one. "That sounds like something Tolkien would write, but the others—"

"They're off. That's why I didn't recognize where they'd come from at first. They're all off."

"What do you mean?"

"Like, this first one. *A hunted man wearies.* What Tolkien actually wrote was that a hunted man sometimes wearies of distrust and that he longs for friendship."

"Okay." Kate drew the word out, took another bite of her burger, then pushed the basket away and picked up the list again. She studied it for several minutes, then placed it carefully back on the table. "Give me another example."

"This second one." She tapped the sheet with her finger. "Meet revenge with revenge? Tolkien wrote something like it's *useless* to meet revenge with revenge. They're all like that—taken out of context."

"Except the last."

"Right."

"I don't know what any of this means."

"Neither do I, but I think they're from John."

"John Howard."

"He's trying to provoke me into making a mistake, or get under my skin, or something. I don't know." Allison sat back and realized she felt better to have this particular puzzle out in the open. Why had she thought she could carry it on her own? When would she learn that working as a team meant suffering and struggling and puzzling things out—together? "What do you think?"

"I don't think those messages are from John Howard."

"Why?"

"He never liked the Tolkien stuff."

"But you said he called his operation center in Montana middle-earth."

"And I originally thought John had picked that name, but the more I worked with him, the more I watched him, the less I believed that. It didn't fit. John focused completely on his mission and was very military in his approach. I don't see him reading high fantasy from the 1950s."

"Then who—"

"Stella. I think it was Stella's idea."

Allison thought of the dream. There had been something different. What was it she had seen?

Suddenly, there was shouting, and Kate stood up. Whatever was happening was occurring up by the order line. Allison joined her and together they left their table and moved closer.

One of the men she'd seen wearing a holster was confronting a customer standing in line. He was wearing jeans and a Bubba Gump Shrimp Co. t-shirt. It wasn't a uniform exactly, but it was plain that he was there to protect the place.

"You don't bring that thing in here unless it's in a pouch."

"Who made you the police?" The teenaged kid couldn't have been over nineteen. He wore his hair long, his jeans low and around his hips.

Allison suspected he was someone passing through the area, Apparently, he had taken his phone out to check his messages while he waited in line.

Bubba wore a shoulder holster and had fifty pounds and ten years on the kid.

"There are signs all over the parking area. You leave it in your car or you put it in a QuantumGuard Pouch."

The name for the small pouches struck Allison as odd. Most people didn't know what a quantum computer was. No one even knew for certain if one actually existed. All of the big tech companies—Google, Apple, even Starlink—claimed to have one in the development phase. Allison had never seen one, and it would seem the U.S. Government's Cyber Task Force would know if such a thing had been built.

Still, the pouches apparently brought a measure of peace to people and were being adopted across the country. Point in case—they were being required in small town Nebraska. Based on what Kate had said earlier, Allison doubted anyone could confirm that they provided one hundred percent protection for the person in possession of the cellular device.

"Maybe I can't afford one." The kid's tone was plaintive, argumentative.

That probably set off Bubba as much as anything else.

"You bought those ridiculous jeans. If you don't have the money to purchase a pouch, you leave the phone in your vehicle. You do not bring it into this place where innocent folk could be collateral damage."

"Or what?"

"Or I'll kick your ass."

"Right."

The teenager stood backed into a proverbial corner, and Allison suspected he'd come out swinging at any moment.

"Why don't you just shoot me? You're wearing a gun. Are you scared to use it?"

"Kid has a death wish," Kate muttered as they moved to intercept.

Kate took the kid.

Allison took the big guy.

"Maybe give him some space," Allison said in a low voice as she stepped in front of him.

"Why would I do that?"

"So he has a minute to consider the wisdom of your words."

At that, the big guy shook his head, looked out over the crowd that was watching, and shrugged. "Sure, but he needs to get that thing out of here. There are families eating dinner. Kids."

"Right."

Their eyes met, and Allison could feel him take the measure of her.

"Why do you care?" he asked. "You're not from here."

"I'd rather not get caught up in a police investigation."

"As if," the big guy said. "We have three local cops, and they're usually on the highway giving tickets."

"Thanks for the warning."

His gaze moved past her to the kid, who was now walking toward the parking lot.

Kate joined them. "He's taking it to his vehicle. Says he tried to buy a pouch on-line, but every place was sold out. I'm Kate, by the way."

Allison followed her lead, using their real names. "I'm Allison."

"Brian." He grudgingly shook their hands. "Do you have cell phones?"

Allison grinned. "Nope. Gave them up."

"I wish more people would." He studied them in the slanting late afternoon light. "You're both carrying."

Allison shrugged, and Kate laughed. "You're asking pretty personal questions for a first date."

A car squealed as it exited the parking lot—a newer model Dodge Challenger. The kid held his left arm out the window, giving the place and Brian a parting gesture.

"Guess he didn't want a burger after all," Kate said.

Brian laughed. "Glad I didn't have to shoot him."

"Would you have done that?" Allison asked.

"Maybe." His expression turned serious. "Things have been tense around here lately."

"Here?" Allison smiled as she gestured toward the food line, the tables filled with families, the games of corn hole and washers being played.

"Yeah. Looks like idyllic rural America, but it's not quite that."

"Something happen?" Kate cocked her head, curled a strand of her hair around her finger and waited. She looked like a college kid when she took that pose.

Brian rolled his eyes skyward, but couldn't stop the slow and steady smile that inevitably came from being flirted with. "Old guy's pacemaker blew up last week. Killed him and injured the dentist who was working on him. Then someone came through town in one of those self-driving cars. It crashed through the front of our only grocery store. Injured six. Guy claimed the computer took over, and he couldn't stop it."

"Is that why you're carrying that Smith and Wesson in a holster?" Allison asked.

"Yeah. Me and a few others. We're just trying to keep people safe."

Allison held out her hand again, and he shook it, a goofy grin spreading across his face.

They were back in the Bronco and four miles down the road before Allison called Kate on her move.

"You were actually using your charms on that guy to decelerate the situation."

"It worked."

"Yes, it did."

They started laughing. It felt good. Nothing about the situation at the burger joint had been funny, but then nothing about the state of the country was funny either. The laughter was probably born of stress and exhaustion and still, it felt good.

"Why did you use your real name?" Allison asked.

Kate glanced at her, then turned her attention to the road. "That guy? Bubba?"

"Brian."

"Right. Brian. He would have spotted a lie before it was completely out of my mouth."

"You're probably right. He was astute."

"Goes to show you can't judge country people by their looks."

"Bubba Gump. I can't believe they still sell those t-shirts. That movie has to be twenty years old."

"More than that. Came out in 94."

"Are you a movie buff?"

"I might have watched it a few times."

Allison wanted to enjoy the moment, relax, talk about old movies. Instead, she pulled out the road atlas and calculated the distance. "Seven hours to go."

"Could have taken a plane."

"And yet I'm glad we didn't."

"Same."

Which nicely summed up their situation. Do it the hard way. Do it right. Hope they came out ahead of John Howard and the AT. Hope that this time they could stop the madness before it even began.

Kate dropped her bags on the bed of her room in the Creekside Lodge. She wanted to fall on the mattress and pass out, but she knew once she did, she'd be gone for at least eight hours. There were a few things she needed to set up first.

They were on the second floor of the lodge. Donovan's room was on the end, Kate's was next to it, and Allison's was the third room from the end of the hall. She understood that Allison's room would be empty—she'd be bunking with Donovan. The extra room gave them a buffer against anyone attempting to listen in on what they were doing. It was a solid plan.

She stepped out onto the balcony because she needed the fresh air to wake her up. The Milky Way stretched out above her as if she were seeing it in a planetarium. She closed her eyes, heard the call of an owl, the short, sharp bark of a fox, then complete silence. Custer State Park encompassed 71,000 acres set in the Black Hills and—according to the pamphlet she'd picked up at the registration desk—included prairies, forests, mountains, and lakes. Plus, tourists had a good chance of seeing a fairly substantial herd of bison, longhorn antelope, prairie dogs, deer, bighorn sheep, and wild burros. Something told Kate she wouldn't have the chance to see most of those things.

She and Allison had stopped at a 24-hour cafe outside of Custer and ordered breakfast. That had been at three a.m. There had been no way to contact Donovan, so they'd stalled over cups of coffee, then added a piece of pie to the breakfast they'd quickly consumed. Kate might have worried about the caffeine in the coffee, but it was a weak blend, and she didn't think anything could have kept her awake once she finally put her head on a pillow.

When they calculated they'd given Donovan plenty of time to scout out the lodge and set up the rooms before them, they drove the remaining miles to Custer State Park. The hills loomed in the darkness, and the stars covered the night sky above them. She'd never seen so many, not even in Whitefish.

"Have you ever been here?"

"Once," Allison said. "With my dad."

Kate understood that what Allison had been through, seeing her father killed at the tender age of nine, hiding for hours and then walking down that mountain alone—it had all changed her friend. It had shaped her.

And perhaps the same could be said for Kate.

Both of her parents had passed while she was in college—a car crash when someone had crossed the dividing line and hit them head on. Her sudden aloneness in the world had probably been what prompted her to take a job with Homeland Security. Making fistfuls of money with a private organization held little appeal. Kate didn't need the money. She had her parents' life insurance, which was enough to set her up for life. She didn't want to be set up for life. She'd so much rather be able to pick up a phone and call her pop, meet her mom for lunch, go home for Thanksgiving and Christmas.

Instead of joining the private sector, she'd taken a job with Homeland Security and because she had no siblings and no parents—no actual family to speak of—she'd been able to throw herself into the job. She'd actually been eager to accept the undercover assignment. She still hadn't recovered completely from that particular hell, but terrorism marched on, and she'd only taken three weeks off before jumping into the fray again.

She breathed in the cool, fresh air, which was a relief after the humidity of Kansas. She understood why they had to do everything low tech, but the drive had been exhausting. Miles of flat land. Miles of open vistas spotted only with the occasional farm. It had reminded her that there was a lot of America out there—miles and miles of small towns and good people and unspoiled countryside. But it had also made her anxious to get to work.

Computers were what she knew.

Coding was what she did.

Kate's first task was to set up the portable Faraday cage she'd brought. She'd already placed the *Do Not Disturb* sign on the door, but should anyone walk in, they'd basically see what looked like clear plastic panels positioned around the room's desk. The panels were incredibly thin and had folded down to the size of a notebook. When spread out, they became more rigid, forming a cyber shield around her workspace. She placed the second black bag on the desk and pulled her laptop from it. The laptop itself was air-gapped. From her pocket, she retrieved what looked like a USB drive. It was in effect a mobile hotspot that bounced off three international servers before accessing the Task Force's mainframe. It was impenetrable and quite expensive which explained why everyone on the Task Force didn't have one. Even task forces answered to the accounting department. The public's perception of black ops with unlimited budgets might be correct, but she'd never experienced it.

The air-gapped computer had been provided by the task force.

The special USB device she'd purchased on the black market. If this op went well, maybe the task force would reimburse her for it. If not, there went her nest egg.

She'd spend her last dollar if it allowed her to stop the AT. Kate had worked in middle-earth for two years. It had been dreadful and eye-opening, terrifying and at times—a bit of a rush. John lured in the very best programmers whose services were auctioned to the highest bidder. John outbid everyone—Google, Apple, Microsoft. Amazon, Meta, and Tesla. The result wasn't the most well adapted bunch, but they were very good. There had been brief moments—between the instances of terror—when she'd enjoyed working with them.

Kate was good, too. She wasn't arrogant. She simply understood what she brought to the table, in the same way that Donovan knew his size would sometimes be an advantage and Allison knew that her passion gave her an added edge. Kate's coding skills were excellent, but it was her memory that set her apart. She knew that there was no one in John Howard's employ who could hack into this set-up.

It would take the laptop over an hour to receive updates from the Task Force, and then it would shut itself down. Stepping out of the Faraday cage, she stripped out of her clothes, walked to the suite's bathroom, and took a twenty-minute shower. Washing off the grime of the road helped her feel better and even more tired. She toweled off, donned the hotel's robe, and walked back into the Faraday cage, where she confirmed the update was at forty-eight percent.

She exited the cage, retrieved her Sig Sauer and set it on the table next to her bed, pulled back the covers, turned off the light, and fell immediately into a deep sleep.

Kate woke six hours later to sunlight pouring through the gap in the curtains and the sound of Allison banging on her room's door.

Chapter Four

John Howard realized he should have been pleased.

The chaos at Los Angeles International Airport was spectacular. The story streamed in a continual loop on every news channel. Even entertainment channels led with the *breaking story*, and it held the top hashtag position on X.

#LAXDOWN

Indeed, it was down.

Los Angeles International Airport provided flights for more than seventy-five million customers per year. It was the world's eighth largest airport and served as a major international gateway to Asia, Mexico and Central America.

"Over five hundred injured," Jasmine reported in a voice devoid of emotion. "All concourses have been shut down. EMS is responding. Local and federal agents are in route."

John rarely allowed himself satisfaction regarding their work. There was always something they could have done better, some small repercussion they hadn't planned for. But this looked like a bang-up job. It had been Spencer's idea to hack into airport security's walkie-talkies. Exploding them had been as easy as exploding the smart phones. John was tempted to crack out the champagne.

"Have you found her?" Stella's voice interrupted John's momentary celebration. Her pitch and tone grated on his nerves worse than fingernails on a chalkboard. He turned to scowl at her. Today his boss wore a green silk outfit that would have fit perfectly into the Wizard of Oz.

Spencer fielded the question. "There's been no movement on Allison Quinn's cell phone, passport, or task force I.D."

"I doubt she's just sitting at home enjoying this on her big screen."

John's temper flared. "What difference does it make? We're making history here. Look at the stock prices of every major airline." He stormed over and gestured adamantly toward a screen showing the DOW ticker. Why couldn't Stella see this was a success? Combined with the events of the next twenty-four hours, he felt real optimism that they could succeed in reversing the ambivalence of the American people.

Stella wasn't buying it. "Where is Donovan Steele? Find him, and we'll likely find her."

"Agent Steele is at a hospital in Virginia with a leg break—compound fracture that actually punctured the skin." Spencer tapped on his keyboard bringing up a picture of the agent. "We hacked into his medical chart. They're prepping him for surgery this morning—plates, screws, rods—he's getting it all. We even sent a third party to verify it was him."

"And what of Kate Jackson? Am I to believe that she's simply fallen off the grid as well? Traded in her coding skills to become a homemaker? Maybe she decided to vacation abroad for a few years."

No one dared to answer that. Kate Jackson had disappeared into the night. She'd become less than a vapor. They'd run what they had on her through every government and private surveillance system. Nothing. Not even a blip.

"I want the three of them. I want to see them with my own

eyes and kill them with my own hands. This—" Her voice shook as she waved toward the monitors. "This is not a success until I have confirmed that Donovan, Quinn, and Jackson are dead. Do you understand?"

She stormed from the room. Maybe to drink more in private. Possibly to apply another layer of poisonous frog polish to her nails. John didn't care.

He moved to the front of the room. "Our focus remains on the sequence of events we have scheduled for the next thirty-eight hours."

The words were barely out of his mouth when every screen in the room went black. His pulse quickened, and he barked orders even as his mind tried to come up with a scenario that did not spell unmitigated disaster. His five programmers moved from screen to screen. A few dropped to the floor to see if the problem could be cables, but John Howard knew it was nothing that simple.

All communication systems were down.

The lights flickered and then they, too, went out.

He heard Stella screech his name and beyond that the rat-a-tat-tat of machine gun fire. The attack that he'd been expecting for years was finally upon them. His people had drilled for this very scenario. In Whitefish they'd had a little time to move what was critical and destroy what was left behind, but he'd known that if they were tracked down again there would be no mercy.

And mercy wasn't what he wanted.

What he wanted was to win.

Three of the programmers stood by their workstations, dumbfounded expressions coloring their faces as they stared at their blank screens. He shot them point-blank. After that, the remaining two started moving quickly to disassemble their drives.

"Leave them," John barked.

The guards outside would either hold off the enemy or surrender to them. It didn't matter.

"Jasmine, put the back-up drives into one of the go bags.

Spencer, grab three of the hardened laptops and put them in the other bag. Both of you find Stella and see that she gets to the safe room in the basement." He pushed a button on his watch. "I'll meet you there in two minutes."

He didn't say inane things you'd probably hear in a star-studded box-office release.

He did not caution them to *be careful.* Of course, they would be careful. Their lives were on the line.

He certainly didn't bother with *don't leave me.* They didn't know how to leave him. John was the only one who knew how the tunnel constructed under the mansion worked. He had been the only one to meet with the DeepWay Solutions CEO. No one else was even aware of the tunnel's existence. He'd made sure of that.

He dashed to his room, grabbed his personal go bag from the closet, pulled what looked like a small, hard shell suitcase from under his bed, opened it and slapped his palm to the screen, quickly setting the timer to three minutes. Satisfied to see the detonation clock begin to tick down, he shoved aside the device, unzipped a secret pocket on his mattress, and removed what looked like a car fob. His handprint should be enough, but he considered it prudent to have a backup plan. There was always the possibility that his adversaries had released an EMP, in which case he'd need a key to start the vehicle's engine.

Finally, he moved aside a curtain and pressed the elevator button. Making sure his room held the only private elevator access to the basement had been smart. In a part of his mind, he realized there was a difference between planning in general for an event, and preparing every step of his needed departure as if such a thing was inevitable.

Subconsciously, he had known this day would come.

The elevator descended smoothly. When he stepped out into the basement's anteroom, he turned north and headed straight for the long corridor that sloped down, down, down and then curved left. A dozen yards ahead, he caught a flash of emerald green color

—Stella's ridiculous silk skirt. When the ceiling above him shook, he knew that the charges he'd set had gone off. A terrific roar and the sound of the structure crumbling followed the shaking over their heads.

John Howard didn't slow down.

He didn't pause to look over his shoulder, but continued at a brisk pace until he'd caught up with their little group of merry men—and women, of course. He wasn't a troglodyte.

Jasmine and Spencer each carried two heavy go-bags. They looked terrified—their complexion pale, their gaze jumping from one thing to another, their mouth slightly open as if they couldn't believe what they were seeing. Maybe they couldn't. Everyone who worked for John was aware of the basement safe room, but they'd only been shown the location, a cursory look of the ante-room, a glimpse of the long hall. Only John had actually walked down the corridor that branched out from the room.

His top two programmers might be terrified, but Stella Gonzalez was not. She looked irritated, as if the entire sequence of events had inconvenienced her.

Thankfully, all three of them remained silent.

For John, events were unfolding exactly as he'd expected. He'd run this scenario over in his mind every night since first aligning his fight with Stella's. Instead of being concerned, he had the exhilarating feeling of finally being able to live out an oft repeated dream.

The lights flickered, causing Spencer to gasp.

The walls shook again and Jasmine flinched away from them.

Stella sniffed the air, shrugged, and pierced John with a glare.

John ignored all of them and pushed his way to the panel inset into the wall next to the nearly invisible door. The seams of the door matched up perfectly with the wall. If you hadn't known they were there, you wouldn't have immediately seen them. The panel itself wasn't visible until John waved his hand at the precise location—eighteen inches above waist level, six inches to the right of the door frame.

The panel glowed red. He pressed his fingertips against it, and the door opened. No one questioned what to do. Fire alarms continued to blare. The sound of additional explosions reached them though they were thirty feet underground. They needed to get out of Dodge—and fast.

Their escape transportation waited for them at the entry to the tunnel. A soft light came up from the floor and extended a dozen yards beyond where it sat. There was barely enough space between the vehicle and the tunnel walls to open the doors.

"I'm not getting into that," Jasmine said.

"Fine. Stay." John grabbed both of her go bags and threw them into the trunk of the car. Once Spencer had done the same, he slammed the compartment shut.

Jasmine, understanding that she was about to be left, got into the back seat of the car. Spencer sat beside her. Stella didn't bother calling shotgun—it was plain that she expected the best seat in the vehicle. Leg room was important to a lady, though as she climbed inside she looked even more unnerved.

"I'm not sure I trust you to drive us into a tunnel with less than a foot of clearance on either side."

"Who said I was driving?" John touched the ignition, relaxed slightly at the roar of the engine, and engaged the autonomous pilot of the Voltaris X.

"This car isn't supposed to exist," Spencer said. "It's supposed to be under review by the NHTSA and the FCC."

"Yup. Better buckle up." John had only driven the vehicle twice —once above ground and the second time in the tunnel. Neither time had he approached the top speed of the Voltaris X which had broken records by achieving 317 mph. The vehicle was fully autonomous, featured four electric motors which generated over 2,000 horsepower, and could achieve zero to sixty miles per hour in 1.6 seconds.

The lead engineer for the next generation EV had explained that the acceleration would be comparable to three times the normal gravitational force. In other words, they were about to experience three times their body weight pressing against their torso.

John had always dreamed it would be the ride of a lifetime.

The reality was even better.

He felt his body pushed back against the seat. Found he couldn't turn his head left or right. Did his vision blur? Possibly, and he had a hard time pulling in a deep breath. He focused on the control panel, his vision cleared, and he watched the mph gauge climb from 100 to 150 to 200. Adrenaline coursed through his brain, and he wanted to laugh.

He wanted to shout, "Yes!"

A momentary sense of satisfaction flickered through him. So their hand had been forced. What an exhilarating experience! Plus, they had prevailed.

Then the lights of the tunnel flickered before going out completely. He had the fleeting thought that something was wrong as they hurled through the darkness at three hundred miles per hour.

What was happening at LAX was a tragedy, but Allison understood it was also a distraction.

"If that's true, if his only intention was to pull agents from ongoing Homeland Security ops, I'd say John Howard has definitely attained the status of overachiever." Donovan steepled his fingers and continued staring at the television screen.

They couldn't all fit inside the portable Faraday cage, so instead Donovan and Allison sat on the end of the king-sized bed while Kate sat in the cage, monitoring the direct feeds she'd put in place earlier. Donovan had the television controller in his hand and channel surfed between news stations.

Allison put a hand on his arm when she saw a familiar figure step to the news podium—Kenneth Langston, Director of

Homeland Security. Kate glanced up, saw what they were watching, stepped out of the cage, and stood beside them.

The crowd of reporters quieted.

Langston didn't begin speaking immediately. Neither did he look down at notes. Instead, he allowed his eyes to scan the room as if to assure himself that the people who needed to be in attendance were.

With a slight nod, he began. "At fourteen minutes after nine this morning, a debilitating cyber-attack hit Los Angeles International Airport. Although the bulk of the damage affected on-line systems, the resulting chaos caused many civilian deaths. Malfunctions encompassed all people-transport systems including moving walkways, shuttle buses, escalators, and monorails."

It seemed to Allison that his expression grew even more severe and his knuckles might have whitened on the podium.

"Over half a dozen terrorist groups—both domestic and foreign—have claimed responsibility for today's attack. We believe this deluge of possible assailants is one more way the real culprits hope to get away with what they've done."

Now he paused.

Stared down at the podium.

Finally, looked up again.

"They will not get away with what they've done. We will find them. We will hold them responsible. They will see their day in a U.S. court where they will face prosecution to the full extent of the law. However, that day is not today. In order to ensure the safety of American travelers, we are temporarily ordering the closure of all U.S. airports, both private and public."

His last sentence produced a cacophony of questions from the reporters.

He raised his right hand, and they all fell silent.

"We've been through a similar situation before, folks. After the events of 9-11, all flights were cancelled for nearly two days. This time, we will also close metro rails and subways in all major U.S. cities. We will harden these systems, guarantee that they are inaccessible from any rogue players, and then gradually allow providers to resume their operation."

"Director Langston—" someone shouted, but he had no chance to get out his question.

"This will not be easy. Our enemies may be able to shut down transportation systems, but they will not shut down this country. You will need to carpool. You'll need to walk. You'll need to work from home if you can and make alternate transportation plans if you can't. If someone has a bicycle, borrow it. If someone needs transportation to your part of the city, offer them a ride."

He paused again, and Allison realized HS had not expected this. They'd been so focused on the explosions of individual tech devices that they hadn't expected or prepared for a one-two punch.

"Make no mistake. This is war, and we will treat it as such. The President will speak about that aspect of this event during his news conference later today. In the meantime, you need to know that all ride-sharing companies have been temporarily nationalized. We will make sure that people can reach hospitals, that emergency responders can get to work, that anyone in a business essential to the health and well-being of the people of this country will have transportation."

He stepped away from the podium without answering a single question, turned, and strode from the room. The Secretary of Transportation stepped forward and began fielding questions.

Donovan muted the television.

Allison saw the surprise and anger and grief she was feeling reflected in the eyes of her friends. How many people had to die at the hands of John Howard? And she had no question that it was John Howard and the Anarchists for Tomorrow who were behind the attack. The question was, why did he seem to always be one step ahead of them?

That wasn't all she saw in her friends' expressions, though.

She also saw the same resolve she felt.

"Let's put it to a vote," Donovan suggested. "We can answer the call that is scrolling on Kate's screen..."

They turned as one to see the scrolling alert now running on the bottom of all government computers.

ALL HOMELAND SECURITY EMPLOYEES ARE TO REPORT TO THEIR SUPERVISOR IMMEDIATELY. ALL VACATIONS ARE HEREBY CANCELLED. IF YOU CANNOT REPORT....

"We can answer that call," Donovan said. "Or we can stay our course."

"Which could mean getting fired." Kate's eyes sparkled as she wiggled her eyebrows.

And that was exactly what Allison needed to see.

They all understood the seriousness of this situation. But Allison firmly believed that what was about to happen—the single event this was leading up to—would happen at Mount Rushmore.

"We're in the right place here," she said. "The Black Hills. Mount Rushmore. We're where we need to be."

"Agreed." Donovan held out his hand, palm down.

She felt ridiculous, but Allison placed her hand on top of his, and Kate pressed her hand on top of theirs.

"On three," Donovan said.

"Wait. What are we saying?" Kate's smile had widened.

"Game on," Allison whispered.

Which seemed to sum it up nicely.

They understood this wasn't a game. They were painfully aware of lives sacrificed not only that morning but stretching back to that terrible encounter in the depths of the Grand Canyon. Stretching back to Allison's father.

Donovan counted, "One. Two..."

And on "Three" they all vowed, "Game on."

Chapter Five

Allison had watched Kate set traps inside of every digital system within the Mount Rushmore National Park. None of them had been tripped. There was virtually no unusual activity, and yet it had to be opening. John Howard lurked nearby. She could practically smell brimstone, smoke, rot, and decay.

Kate sat with her fingertips pressed against her forehead.

"What?" Allison pressed.

They were sitting on the bed with maps Allison had picked up from the front desk of the lodge spread around them.

"I'm missing something."

"Huh."

"You know the feeling?"

"Yeah. I definitely do." Allison wanted to close her eyes against those failures—shove them from her mind.

Donovan warning her about the man killed on the road leading to the park entrance of the Grand Canyon. Tate's eyes locked with hers as she knelt frozen in the middle of the bridge spanning the Colorado River while her acrophobia built, then rose to a crescendo. Zack with a slash across his stomach, exposing tissue and muscles. Donovan nearly bleeding out in the engine room of the *Harmony of Dreams*.

She wanted to push those memories away, but she also understood that they could serve to make her more careful this time. "I definitely do know the feeling."

They studied the maps, access points, main roads, secondary roads, delivery entrances. Donovan had even snagged an aerial map.

"I've never longed so fiercely for Google Earth," Kate said.

Allison wasn't much of a programmer. She'd always excelled on the field work side of things. Her training had included writing code, tweaking programs, spotting intruders. She understood that the use of Google Earth or any real-time satellite data exponentially increased their likelihood of being noticed—either by John Howard's programmers or by a traitor within their own organization. A Faraday cage could keep their system from being compromised, but any data going in or out could be snatched.

It shouldn't happen.

But it could.

"This is going to sound crazy." Allison scooted so that her back rested against the headboard of the bed. Her bare feet stretched out in front of her.

Anyone glancing in the room would see two women who looked to be planning the next steps of their vacation. They'd never suspect two government agents overseeing the biggest op of their career. Okay, if they saw the Faraday cage, they might grow suspicious, but otherwise Allison suspected the scene would appear normal, mundane even.

She picked up a map, studied it, then tossed it back on the pile. "What if the AT goes low tech?"

"I'm not following."

"They're expecting us to watch the code."

"Maybe at the twenty-four locations that the Task Force picked."

"The AI program picked those."

"The Task Force and the AI program worked in tandem. John could have run the same programs on his end. He could have anticipated our prediction and decided to go low tech. I could see that happening there, but not here." Kate worried a thumbnail. "They're not expecting us here—in South Dakota, in the middle of nowhere. We're 380 miles from an international airport."

"True, though there is an airport in Rapid City which is just a few miles—"

"Regional airport. It doesn't have the appeal of an international airport. Literally, no one else would or did pick Mount Rushmore as the site for the AT's big event because it's not a solid target."

"No one except you and I." Allison met her friend's gaze. Kate had spent over two years working for John Howard. Allison had spent all her life looking for him because she was very sure that he had killed her father, or at least he'd had a hand in it.

"Right. We picked it for several reasons." Kate ticked them off on her fingers, as if needing to remind herself of why they were planning an op in the lodge of Custer State Park. "It's a symbol of our nation."

"Don't forget it displays the heads of four presidents."

"It's a monument to democracy. A cultural and historical legacy."

"All true, though that doesn't make this spot unique. America has many monuments to democracy."

"Plus, big tourism, especially on the fourth of July." Kate threw up her hands. "It's patriotic. You can almost hear the National Anthem fanning out over the Black Hills."

Allison tapped the brochure, showcasing the Crazy Horse Memorial.

"What about here?" She waved the brochure. "It's controversial. I think that John Howard sees himself as equal to the most famous Lakota Sioux warrior. Maybe he thinks he's fighting the Battle of the Little Bighorn all over again. Of course, he thinks this time he'll win."

"Yeah." Kate leaned forward, elbows on knees, and studied the tourist pamphlet for the Crazy Horse Memorial. "He always had a grandiose opinion of himself."

"Don't all martyrs?"

"There we disagree. I don't see John as a martyr. A martyr stands their ground, but John will turn tail and run in a minute. His primary goal is to live and fight another day."

Which reminded Allison of what she shared in common with John Howard. They had both lost their family. "Did he ever talk to you about his wife and child?"

"Not really. I think he mentioned it a few times to Brett Lindstrom. Brett told me once that John thought of himself as David fighting Goliath."

"Interesting that he would use a Biblical example."

"John had a solid career in military intelligence as well as the CIA. Solid until a foreign assassin murdered his wife and daughter, in this country." Kate pulled her hair back, gathering it with her hands as if the weight of it on her neck suddenly bothered her. "That tragedy pushed him over the edge."

"Which is understandable."

"But killing other innocent people to get even? That is not understandable. It doesn't make sense that he would attempt to ease the pain of his own loss by creating so much additional pain in the world."

"The kind of people we chase, and hopefully apprehend, they don't make sense." Allison understood what Kate was struggling with. The why of it. The nonsensical nature of what truly desperate people did. "We have no hope of understanding him, and maybe that's okay. Maybe we don't want to experience his frame of mind in any way. What remains true is our mission."

"And how would you describe that?"

"At its most basic? Protection of the Republic."

"We have to find him." Whatever Kate was struggling with, her resolve overcame it. "We have to find him because I don't think John Howard will stop short of complete capitulation of the U.S. Government. He'll run, but he'll always return to the fight."

"Agreed."

They both stared at the image of the still-in-progress Crazy Horse Memorial.

"It'll be harder," Allison said. "Covering two sites with three people, but I think we need to do it. I think that somehow not doing it will be a regret farther down the road."

"Agreed. And look!" A smile spread across her face as she pointed to a line on the brochure which read *Live Webcams*. "Bet I can hack into those."

"While you do that, I'll make notes of the secondary roads."

"Also compile information on the helicopters that provide tourist rides. I wouldn't put it past the AT to use one of the local services to deliver their destruction."

"I'm on it."

When Donovan joined them an hour later, they explained the plan, the schedules they'd come up with, the surveillance they wanted to complete immediately.

"It's a lot." Donovan stared down at the plans, then his glance skipped up to Kate and over to Allison. "Are you both sure you don't want to call in backup?"

The television was still on, though the sound was muted. Images of airports and subways around the nation—all closed—played across the screen, interrupted only by updated death and casualty numbers. Some people had been trampled. Others had tumbled headfirst down escalators. A few had jumped to their death from monorails, apparently convinced the computer driven rides were about to explode.

Calling in additional agents would mean pulling people away from those locations. If the conclusions they'd made were wrong, that would be a terrible move to make. And if they were right, pulling in more people would most certainly attract attention from the AT.

"We do this alone," Allison said.

No one argued.

"One more thing," Kate said. "According to everything I've found, the Hall of Records is completely inaccessible."

"What Hall of Records?" Donovan asked.

"You want to tell him?"

Allison shrugged. "Originally designed by Gutzon Borglum to be eighty by one hundred feet and adorned with a large inscription. At one time there was even talk of putting the original Constitution there."

"I thought that was a myth," Donovan said.

"Nope." Kate shook her head, causing her thick black hair to sway back and forth. "They started working on it in 1938."

"But Congress nixed the idea in 1939. In 1998 workers completed a simpler version."

"There's an actual tunnel at Mount Rushmore? Where?"

"Behind Lincoln's head. Like I said—inaccessible."

"How inaccessible?"

"According to everything I've been able to dig up—some public, some not—there's a teakwood box, inside a titanium vault, covered by a granite capstone. There are no cameras on that portion of the site. I brought it up because I suppose there's a small chance Howard found a way to use it."

"To what end?"

"I don't know. Shoot rockets from it? Howard's hubris knows no limit, but he's also practical. I don't think he'd risk it, but you might keep an eye open while you're there."

"Got it."

They stood, checked their packs and their weapons. Kate did something inside the Faraday cage, then smiled. Allison wasn't a tech pro. But she understood that if anyone attempted to enter the makeshift device, they wouldn't be walking away with information. They might not be walking away at all.

Allison turned up the volume on the television. Donovan made sure the drapes were completely closed. Kate confirmed the *Do Not Disturb* sign was in place as they closed the door.

They stepped out of the lodge into a perfect summer day. The colors seemed almost too bright—the deep blue of the sky, the green of the pine-covered hills, the browns and blacks and grays of the granite peaks in the distance.

The Black Hills were quintessentially American, and Allison remained convinced that this was where the AT would strike. It was unblemished, beautiful, reminiscent of what their great country had looked like so long ago. In fact, from where they were walking across to the parked vehicles, very little around her had changed in the last hundred years. A sliver of a road. Some cabins by the river. National Park employees leading a group of tourists.

But no cell towers she could see.

No oil or gas wells pumping.

No wind turbines.

John Howard was pining for a time before his life had taken a turn toward the tragic. And in the same way, he would look for a place that exemplified the same pre-corrupted era of America. This was it. This was where he would attack.

It was time to do some reconnaissance.

The distance between the lodge at Custer State Park and Crazy Horse Memorial was nineteen miles. Twenty from the lodge to Mount Rushmore, but in the opposite direction.

Kate drove the Bronco toward Crazy Horse. Donovan had arrived in a 1962 Volkswagen bus. He and Allison took that vehicle to Mount Rushmore. Both vehicles were old enough to be completely devoid of technology. Neither could reach a top speed over seventy. She supposed if it came down to a car chase, things would already be careening toward disaster.

The two sites were only sixteen miles apart, and tracing a path from the lodge to both of them would have resulted in a slightly wobbling circle through the Black Hills. Kate took US-16 west through the small town of Custer, pausing only long enough to grab a fresh coffee and a banana. She needed both the caffeine and the calories. She also needed a good night's sleep. The five hours she'd managed the night before had helped, but she could feel her energy waning.

She made a right onto US-385 N, and that was when things grew more interesting. She'd expected a bit of traffic due to it being July 3rd, but this was not that. Scores of drivers had pulled over and parked haphazardly at the side of the road—too many to be caused by an animal sighting. Even a black bear wouldn't attract that much attention.

She parked the Bronco on the far side of the crowd, not wanting to get blocked in, then trotted toward the group of onlookers. Most held up phones toward the surrounding hills, only a few were in QuantumGuard pouches. They were obviously recording. A few used digital camcorders. She faced the direction they were all pointed in and felt her breath catch in her chest.

Not because what they were gawking at was so inexplainable, but because she thought it had John Howard written all over it. She'd seen one before on the news. Never in person.

"Pretty cool, right?" This from a gray-haired woman wearing a peasant dress, her long hair braided down her back. "We've never had one in South Dakota before."

"How long has it been here?" Kate asked.

"Wasn't here last night when I was driving south." A trucker with his hands stuck into the back pockets of his faded jeans shrugged before shaking his head, pulling off his Sioux Falls Canaries baseball cap, and resettling it on his head. The guy was clearly uncomfortable with the current situation. "At least there were no cars pulled over last night to stare at the damn thing. I drive this route twice a day. Last night I came through about nine-thirty. I suppose it might have been here, but no one had noticed it yet."

"Wasn't here." This from a teenager holding a motorcycle helmet in one hand, his cell phone in the other. "I stop here every night on my way home. Work in Hill City but live in Custer. This spot has the best reception. Definitely wasn't here."

They all turned to stare at the monolith. It appeared to be ten to twelve feet tall. The object's exact dimensions were difficult to calculate since it had been placed nearly a hundred yards away from the road. The Black Hills rose behind the parking area, fell away to the sides, and in the middle sat the reflective structure.

"Dig this," the kid said. He turned his back and held the cell phone down to shade the display from the late morning sun. He pinched the screen, enlarged the picture with his fingertips, then held it out triumphantly for them to see.

The older woman leaned forward and murmured something about aliens.

The truckdriver simply grunted.

Kate focused on memorizing the cipher displayed on his screen. She had no pen, no paper, and no phone of her own to take a picture of the picture, but she had an extraordinary memory—especially for numbers and symbols, something that had come in handy when coding. She asked if she could take a closer look, the kid passed her the phone, and she committed the sequence to memory. Once she was back in the Bronco, she pulled a pad of paper and pen from the pack she'd brought and wrote the message inscribed on the monolith.

She stared at what she'd written, closed her eyes, and finally corrected first one letter, then two, until she was sure she had it exactly as it had been on the screen of the teen's phone. Exactly as it had been on the monolith.

Brx duh vwloo ehlqj olhg wr

Once she understood it was a Caesar cipher, solving it only took her three tries. She stared down at the message, knew it was from the AT, and wondered what it meant.

Then she stuffed the paper and pen back into her pack and

continued toward Crazy Horse. Something told her the monolith wouldn't be the only strange thing she was going to see that day.

The parking area to the memorial brimmed with vehicles. She'd expected as much. Traveling as a Joint Cyber Task Force member, she could have zoomed to the front of the line of cars waiting to pass through the ticket lines. She wouldn't have shown her government ID even if she had it, which she didn't. The point was to do this thing off the radar. She waited impatiently as the line slowly crept forward, grateful for the relatively cold air pushed out by the Bronco's old air conditioner. When she'd made it through the line and parked, she pulled her fake press credentials from the pack, once again fetched the pad and pen, zipped the pack shut and wound her arms through the straps. Her service firearm was in a holster around her ankle. As far as she'd been able to ascertain, there weren't any metal detectors going in to the memorial.

And indeed, getting inside was relatively easy since she'd paid fifteen bucks to the parking attendant. Folks were queuing up for a bus tour. She passed that line and walked toward the memorial, which was astonishing. Reading that someone was attempting to create the largest sculpture in the world into the granite rock face of the mountain was one thing. Seeing it was something else entirely.

Kate looked at the face of Crazy Horse and realized that Allison had been correct. John Howard wouldn't be able to resist comparing himself to the Lakota Sioux leader.

She made her way through the welcome center, museum, and restaurant, noting the location of security cams and trying to see the entire campus through John Howard's eyes. She briefly scanned the gift shop and the cultural center. None of it felt right. None of it felt big enough. Then she stepped outside and her gaze again rose to the sculpture itself.

The monument was huge. The face and arm of Crazy Horse were easily discernible, with the face standing 87.5-feet-tall, as opposed to Mount Rushmore, where each president's face was approximately 60-feet-tall. The sculpted heads of Washington, Jefferson, Roosevelt and Lincoln could all fit inside the area of Crazy Horse's head.

A plaque informed her that the location in front of her was known as Thunderhead Mountain, sacred land according to the Oglala Lakota. The final dimensions for the memorial were planned to be 641 feet long and 563 feet high. Korczak Ziolkowski had begun the work in 1948 and his grandsons continued it to the present day. What a legacy.

John Howard's legacy was going to be quite different.

The completed monument would show Crazy Horse pointing forward, riding a horse. The pointing hand, again according to the plaque, represented Crazy Horse's words, "My lands are where my dead lie buried."

Where my dead lie buried

She stared at the monument for a few more minutes, noting the hole that had been blasted through the mountain, revealing a bright blue sky. That part of the design represented a gap between the arm of the Lakota Sioux warrior and the neck of the horse that would be sculpted beneath him.

She made her way back toward the front of the tourist complex and stopped in front of the small building with a sign reading, "Tour Tickets Here."

"Sorry, ma'am. It's one of our busiest days of the year. We're all sold out."

Kate flashed her press badge, but he was shaking his head before she'd properly shown it to him.

"I wish I could help you."

"Will you be open tomorrow?"

"Yes, we will. Three hundred and sixty-five days a year."

"Thank you."

She thought about walking around the small barrier that allowed buses through, but decided it would be better not to risk it. They could come back later that night, when the crowds were gone. Under the cover of darkness, they could look for any sign that John Howard or the AT had been on the premises.

The effect of the caffeine and carbs rapidly drained away, leaving her yawning and blinking her eyes. She needed to get back to the lodge and sleep for a few hours. Something told her there wouldn't be much chance to do that over the next forty-eight hours. As she climbed into the Bronco, she smiled, thinking of the agent in charge of her initial training. The older man had stressed at the end of every class to sleep while you can.

Between classes. Before classes. After classes. Never during classes, which had caused a ripple of laughter through the room.

"You think training is difficult, and it is. But you will be on ops that are far worse."

Sleep when you can.

Because you can't always sleep.

Chapter Six

John Howard kept his speed under eighty once they exited the tunnel, which was only sixteen miles long. Far enough to put them a safe distance away from the government thugs who were even now combing through the ashes of Middle-earth. Actually, the compound in Montana had been Middle-earth. He hadn't been a big fan of Tolkien, but Stella had insisted they be consistent with their naming methods. A quick Google search had convinced John to call the Wyoming compound Rivendell. Apparently, in Tolkien's book, Rivendell was a place of refuge for the leadership. The analogy worked for him.

Rivendell was now a heap of ashes, and they were flying down what passed for a highway in Wyoming. Stella looked surprised to find herself out in the open. How often did she leave the compound? Apparently not often. Why would she? Stella's mission consumed her entire life. John was focused, but he also had an alternate plan for his life. He wasn't a fool or a zealot. He was a man on a mission that he planned to complete before spending the rest of his life in relative luxury. Would that time be spent alone? Sure. The government had ripped his family away from him. They would pay for that. But if he had to be on this pitiful rock of a planet, he might as well live like the top one percenters.

"How much longer?" Stella drummed her long, possibly poisonous fingernails against the arm rest.

"As long as it takes." John realized he sounded sullen. It was what they expected from him. In truth, he was rather enjoying the events of the day. The flight from Rivendell had been invigorating, the Voltaris drove like a dream, and they had a wide-open road before them. A glance at the back seat told him that Tweedledum and Tweedledee had pulled out their cellular devices and were staring down, swiping, color returning to their previously pale complexions.

"Anything?" he barked.

"Scouring the back corridors of the police communication systems now." Spencer sat up straighter, stared at his phone more intently, then tapped it twice. "This is impossible."

Jasmine flicked a gaze at her seatmate's phone, then returned her attention to her own device. "There's an APB out on both Spencer and myself, along with physical descriptions. How could they possibly have descriptions? And where did they get our real names?"

"I suppose because on your days off..." He put a heavy emphasis on the last two words. He'd been against the idea from the beginning. Cyber-criminals didn't need days off to refuel. The activities they pursued should have been energizing enough. "On your days off, you insisted on going into Casper."

"Yes, but—" Spencer was now swiping quickly, with apparently no better news on each subsequent screen. "I wore a disguise."

"Your cowboy hat was hardly a disguise," Jasmine muttered. "At least I knew to stay out of the local coffee shop."

"What is the use in going to town if you can't enjoy a cappuccino?"

"Shut up. Both of you, just shut up." Stella peered into her side mirror. "John has bigger problems to deal with."

The car which had just passed them on the opposite side of the road had indeed executed a quick turn and was now pursuing them with its red lights strobing, marring the beautiful day.

He could have so easily outrun the officer.

Which would have been foolish.

The last thing he needed was an All-Points Bulletin put out on himself. Better to play nice. Or kill the guy. Whichever the moment seemed to call for. He pulled over and told the "kids" in the back to let him do the talking. Both Jasmine and Spencer were now crouched as low in their seats as they could physically slouch, hats pulled down. Jasmine at least had a book to pretend to be interested in. Spencer opted to fake slumber with his face turned away from the officer.

John threw a don't-say-a-word look at Stella.

She used two black nails to pantomime buttoning her lips closed. Maybe they weren't painted with poison. Or possibly the woman had a death wish—he'd long suspected as much.

By the time he'd rolled down his window, his hands in plain view and on the steering wheel at ten and two, he'd figured out how to play this.

The officer was a twenty-something male. He wore a light brown shirt, dark brown tie, and a Smokey Bear-style hat. A silver badge was displayed on his chest. His utility belt held all the requisite items that could stop a criminal, assuming said criminal wasn't driving a car designed to accelerate zero to sixty in 1.6 seconds.

"Officer."

"May I have your driver's license?"

"Of course. Do you mind if I reach into my back pocket to retrieve it?"

The officer nodded once, hands still carefully placed on his belt for ease of access to both the gun and the taser.

John handed over the identification that he'd paid top dollar for. It had come with a complete background package that pegged him as the beneficiary of a tech start-up, which he purportedly sold for millions over twenty years earlier. John had even insisted that his background include a trail of citations. What rich playboy driving a Voltaris would not have a trail of citations?

"Do you know why I pulled you over?"

"I suspect I was speeding, and I apologize. This road..." He gestured to the empty roadway that stretched as far in front and behind as they could see. "Rather begs to be driven fast."

"We take speeding seriously, sir."

"Of course."

"I clocked you going eighty-nine."

"I was trying to keep it at eighty." He put a little sheepishness in his voice.

"Stay in the vehicle, please."

It wasn't until he'd returned with his warning—South Dakota, like any other state, didn't like to anger its biggest tax-paying citizens—that the trooper allowed an admiring gaze to drift over the vehicle.

"Didn't realize these were on the road yet."

"They aren't. Technically."

"Voltaris?"

"X Model."

"Sweet piece of machinery."

"Indeed."

"Keep it under the speed limit."

"I will do that, Officer."

He'd rolled up his window and pulled away before Stella allowed a cackle to escape. Fingernails on chalkboard. He really needed to limit his time with her.

Unfortunately, they'd be keeping very close company for the next thirty-six hours. After that, who knew? He might allow himself to sever their relationship—permanently.

The entry to Mount Rushmore National Park was rather grand compared to other national parks Allison had visited. Why did her job keep dropping her in the middle of America's most beautiful country? Not that those had been pleasant excursions. She'd killed four terrorists within the rugged walls of the Grand Canyon. Another extremist had died at the hand of her fellow accomplices, and one innocent man had been murdered.

Olympia National Park had been little better.

In the midst of that mountain scenery, she and Donovan had fought men intent on collapsing the western communication sector. She'd taken a bullet and nearly froze to death. Donovan had refused to leave her to go for help. Maybe that was when she'd first admitted to herself that she had feelings for him—not that she'd told him.

She hadn't admitted that she cared, really cared, until he lay on a gurney on the deck of the cruise boat, *Harmony of Dreams*. She'd been so frightened then. So terrified that he would die before she could tell him how much he mattered to her. That she cared. That they deserved a chance.

And yet here they were again, approaching one of the most iconic sites in America, and contemplating a kill-or-be-killed scenario. Maybe their fate was set—destined to always be fighting the forces of evil amidst the rugged beauty of America. The thought depressed her.

"What's tumbling around in that brain of yours, Quinn?"

"Our history."

"Our history?" Donovan pulled forward, handed the parking attendant ten dollars, thanked her, then drove to the top of the two story parking garage. When he'd parked, he turned to study her. "Personal or professional?"

"Professional, though they overlap."

"And?"

"It's bleak, disheartening."

A single eyebrow rose, but he motioned for her to continue.

"Look at this place, Donovan. It's amazing. The Black Hills, the patriotic crowds, the monuments to courageous men. We stumble into this place—as we have in the past, wreak havoc—as we always do, then disappear again. That's our history."

"Nope."

Donovan was a big guy. Five-eleven. Muscular. Played the position of linebacker in college. Nothing about him screamed federal agent or cyber team. He was also off-the-charts smart. Probably smarter than Allison, if she were honest with herself. So when he turned in his seat, squirming so that he could sit sideways, waiting until they could look at each other eye-to-eye, she listened.

"Our history is that we win. We stop those intent on harming America."

"We kill."

"If we have to."

He didn't look away. Didn't crack a joke. He simply waited, and she loved that about him. Letting out a sigh, she ran a hand through her curls, wondering if she looked as disheveled as she felt. Had she even glanced in a mirror that day?

"You look fine." Donovan's voice had dropped an octave. "I don't know how, given the circumstances, but you do."

"Are you flirting with me?"

"Yup."

"Nice."

"Yup."

She felt her malaise lift. She had a job to do. They had a job to do. The terrorists' clock was already ticking. She checked her weapon, then leaned forward so she could slip the Glock into the holster she wore at the back of her jeans' waistband. It meant she had to wear a cotton blouse over her t-shirt, and with temps forecasted to reach the 90s, she'd be sweating before she walked to the monument. Which didn't matter. Being uncomfortable in the South Dakota heat was a small price to pay for catching John Howard.

Donovan's weapon of choice was a SIG Sauer P226. He

checked the magazine, slapped it into the weapon, then slipped the SIG into his shoulder holster. He, too, would wear an extra layer of clothing to cover the firearm. Their fake identification was stamped law enforcement, which was more than likely an unnecessary addition to their backstory. South Dakota did not require permits in order to conceal carry. Anyone who could legally possess a firearm could also conceal carry it. As of February 2010, federal law also allowed anyone who could legally carry a firearm to do so inside the park, though there were certain locations within the facility where that wasn't allowed.

"A third of the people in there will be carrying," Donovan said as they exited the Volkswagen and walked toward the entrance.

"Try not to get shot."

"Noted." He put an arm around her shoulder and squeezed.

Allison tolerated it for a moment, then squirmed away, causing Donovan's laugh to ring out across the bright morning. She'd never been comfortable with public displays of affection. "I'm glad you're with me," she said.

"Yeah?"

"Yeah."

As they walked toward the entrance, they noted the placement of CCTV cameras, which Kate had already hacked into. Mount Rushmore also had automated facial recognition technology, though according to their website they used it sparingly and at the discretion of the park manager. Kate had inserted code within that system to alert them if John Howard appeared. The alert would chime back at the hotel, which might be a message received too late, but the alternative was to carry cellular devices which none of them were willing to do. The only way to keep from being tracked was to forego the benefits of carrying said technology themselves.

They continued past the information center, past Carver's Cafe and the gift shop, then down the Avenue of Flags. Fifty-six flags fluttered in the morning breeze. They represented all fifty states, the District of Columbia, three U.S. territories, and two commonwealths. The beautiful sight prompted a feeling of patriotism within Allison.

However, no one was taking pictures along the avenue.

There wasn't a single person looking up to find their state flag. Once past the entrance, they encountered a great crowd of people, most headed in the same direction Allison and Donovan were.

"More people than I expected," she muttered. "And I expected a lot."

"Because of the monolith," a grandmother leading two small children said. "Aren't we lucky that it appeared today? I never thought I'd get to see one."

Allison and Donovan exchanged glances, then pushed through the jostling group of tourists. A tremendous throng of people had formed at the viewing platform, but Allison had no trouble seeing the monolith. Like others she had read about, it appeared to be made of glass. It had been positioned on the slope directly in front of the center of the monument so that the top of the monument appeared to be level with Theodore Roosevelt's chin.

An older gentleman wearing a Vietnam Vet ball cap shook his head in disbelief. "How did they get it over there?"

How did they?

Five hundred feet of rough terrain stretched between the viewing platform and the four presidents carved out of the massive granite outcropping. Dense stands of ponderosa pines, spruce, and evergreen trees surrounded the monument, and although there were trails and walkways, they formed a circle that culminated in a viewing terrace. A person couldn't reach the base of the monument via the trails. Not easily. Allison looked for but didn't see any indication that vehicles or people had recently climbed the rather steep slope leading up to the monument.

Donovan had worn what looked like tourist-style binoculars around his neck. In fact, they were military-grade optics with range finding and night vision capabilities. The pair he now looked through had no Bluetooth communication.

She stepped closer to him.

"Twelve feet tall. Triangular. Some sort of reflective material." He handed her the binoculars.

As she raised them to her eyes, a teenager in front of them turned and shouted. "There's a message."

She didn't see it at first. Tracking to the bottom of the monolith, she moved her gaze slowly up the side facing them and immediately spied the letters. She stared at them for a moment—then two.

Zh zloo vhw brx iuhh

"Got it," she said, handing the optics back to him.

Donovan spent another moment scanning the trails, then shook his head sharply. There were a lot of people around them, but they all seemed to be staring at the monolith. John Howard's people would be monitoring the crowd.

They hurried into the coffee shop, where Allison borrowed a pen and wrote the letters down on a napkin.

"Looks like a cipher," Donovan said.

"Yup."

As they were leaving the coffee shop, they heard a young couple talking about another monolith that had appeared at Crazy Horse. They didn't ask for details. Things were heating up, and Allison had the terrible feeling that they were already behind.

They met with the director of the facility, Clarence Moss, who insisted he couldn't give them more than five minutes. They used their alias credentials which identified them as state law enforcement, created a bogus reason for being on the premises, and tried to feel him out to see if he had any clue about the monolith, John Howard, or the AT. Moss didn't even react. Simply reiterated that he was busy and walked them to the door of his office.

They spent another two hours reconnoitering the trails and checking out every corner of the facility, even asking a few workers about the Hall of Records. Each time they were told that area was closed to the public. "It's even closed to us," one ranger said. "I've worked here twenty-two years, and I've never seen it."

A dead end, or so it seemed.

The trails, however, were teeming with people. Hikers, joggers, even families with young children tripped down the trails —laughing, calling out to one another, taking photos of the Black Hills, the monument, and, of course, the monolith. The cafe and gift shops were full to the brim. Everyone seemed to be in a celebratory mood.

"There's nothing else to see here." A feeling of dread bubbled up in Allison's gut. She had the sinking conviction that she had been right—that the people around her, enjoying the holiday, were in danger. But she couldn't find any specific evidence pointing to how, where, or when that danger would occur. "We should get back."

"Maybe Kate's program will have picked up who did it."

"Doubt it. She would have analyzed that footage before we left this morning."

"Had to have been done at night."

"Agreed."

"So they already had a feedback loop set into the surveillance system."

"And since Kate didn't notice it, that loop was done by one of the top coders in the country. By one of John Howard's coders."

"Yup."

Allison closed her eyes as they drove back to the lodge. The cipher had to be a simple one. A warning of some sort that any amateur sleuth could decipher. After all, a secret message that no one could understand was useless. Her mind wouldn't settle on a solution, though. She tried to relax, to let the answer come to her, but it didn't happen. Her mind slipped from the cipher, to the Tolkien-like messages, to images of the Grand Canyon and the Gulf of Mexico and the monument. Each time she tried to focus on one thing, another thing intruded, and her thoughts scampered away like a rabbit down a trail.

Donovan nudged her shoulder and said, "Catch a look at this."

She sat up, blinking her eyes at the oddly designed car coming toward them. "What is that?"

"Voltaris. You haven't heard of it?"

"I'm not a car magazine kind of girl."

"Right. The Voltaris X is the newest high-end, sports EV." The red sports car approached on the outside of the oncoming lanes. It definitely stood out. The paint was a metallic red that seemed to change color in the sun. Low to the ground with darkly tinted windows and a design that suggested it might have airborne capabilities definitely pegged it as a playboy's or playgirl's toy.

"How much?" Allison asked, turning in her seat to stare at the vehicle as it passed them.

"Half a million? Maybe more? The thing is, they're not on the market yet."

"How do you know that, Steele?"

"Hey. A guy can dream."

"Missing your Corvette?"

He downshifted the VW's gears in order to help the engine crest the next hill, then turned to her with a wolfish smile. "Maybe a little. Someone thought it would be a bad idea for me to bring it, so I'm stuck driving a van that my grandfather might have driven."

"No technology on this baby, though."

"Indeed."

"That vehicle you own has more tech on board than a small business office."

"Yeah. It does." He laughed, and attempted to rev the VW's engine, which only resulted in a faintly disturbing whine and zero increase in speed. With a sigh, he signaled, then moved over into the slow lane.

Donovan had always maintained a perspective of the lighter side of life, even in the middle of a mission. Allison understood that her constant intensity was both a blessing and a curse. The blessing being that she was always ready to take it to the next level. The curse was that other people had to put up with her. It was a miracle that she and Donovan got along at all.

On reaching the lodge, they stopped at the front desk. A young woman who looked as if she'd been on shift for much too long handed them a message. They moved away from the desk and out of earshot.

"Kate's wiped out. She suggests meeting in her room at six, then grabbing some dinner." Allison turned the note over to see if there was anything on the back, but there wasn't. "Says to wake her if there's anything urgent to share."

They stepped into an elevator that was blissfully empty.

"She's got the right idea." Donovan yawned, then pulled her closer to his side. "We should catch some winks while we can."

"Bound to be a long night." Allison tried to ignore the feel of Donovan's hand pushing her hair off her neck, his lips against her skin, his voice in her ear.

But a part of her understood that Kate and Donovan were both right. They did need to rest. They were only guaranteed the time they had at their fingertips. Who knew what the results of tonight's activities would be? Or tomorrow's? Who knew what diabolical plan John Howard had come up with this time—a plan that he was even now unleashing.

What had she missed? If she'd had a computer, she could have gone on-line and tried to research her research, but that would only serve to draw the AT's attention to them.

There was nothing more they could do until both the Crazy Horse and the Mount Rushmore sites officially closed. They would wait for the cover of darkness. The clock was ticking and the event that they were all primed for was moving closer by the moment. The best thing they could do to prepare was recharge.

If she'd had any doubt that they'd picked the right location, that doubt had vanished with the appearance of the monoliths. She hadn't worked out the cipher yet, but she was certain that the message wasn't meant for her. It was meant to provoke the populace. Given the amount of attention the monolith had drawn, that had been successful. The words would translate into some intrepid slogan like the one that had flashed across the screens of the cruise ship the AT had attacked.

But the monolith did more than rev up the tourists. It confirmed that Allison had been correct. This was the place John Howard had set his sights on.

By installing the monolith with a message, the AT had tipped their hand.

John Howard's first mistake.

With any luck, it wouldn't be his last.

Chapter Seven

"It's a simple Caesar Cipher," Kate said. She felt refreshed, energetic, hopeful. The brain fog of earlier that morning was completely gone.

Allison shook her head. "Remind me—"

"Substitution cipher." Donovan grinned. "When I was a kid, I received a monthly magazine in the mail filled with ciphers, cryptograms, logic puzzles, optical illusions. Loved those things. Good times."

When Allison and Kate stared at him, he held up his hands in a surrender gesture. "I was a little geeky, but I was also athletic. Did I ever tell you I played collegiate football? Linebacker position."

Allison rolled her eyes, and Kate laughed as she turned her attention back to the napkin.

"With a Caesar Cipher, each letter is shifted by a fixed number of positions, in this case three. The Crazy Horse cipher appeared as this—

Brx duh vwloo ehlqj olhg wr

"Back up each letter three spaces. The B becomes a Y, the R

becomes an O..." She wrote the deciphered message below the original.

You are still being lied to

"Not terribly original," Allison said. She looked at what Kate had written on her sheet of paper. Then she pulled a paper napkin from her pocket and flattened it with her palm.

They were once again meeting in Kate's room. Allison and Kate sat on the edge of the king-sized bed. Donovan lurked about. At least they were all somewhat rested. Donovan and Allison had slept six hours. Kate had caught nearly seven. She thought they just might be ready for whatever was about to happen, or as ready as one could be.

"Let's see if yours is any more enlightening." Kate pulled the paper napkin closer to her pad of paper.

Zh zloo vhw brx iuhh

"Looks to be a three position shift again."

"How do you know that? What if we're decoding it wrong?"

"We wouldn't get words that make sense. Maybe one or two would translate to actual words, but they wouldn't all make sense. Let's see—"

All three of them bent closer to read what she'd written.

We will set you free

"Why does that sound more like a threat than a promise?" Allison ran her fingers through her hair.

"Because it is a threat." Donovan plopped into the chair next to the small table. "Let's go over what we know. Someone hacked into the Mount Rushmore security system and put it into a loop so their presence while installing the monoliths wouldn't be detected. The other monolith was left in the vicinity of Crazy Horse, but not on the premises. Why?"

"Maybe they hoped placing it near the side of a major road would attract more attention," Kate said.

"That could be it," Allison said. "Presumptions can be limiting though. Maybe the side of the road wasn't their first choice. Maybe they couldn't hack into the Crazy Horse security system."

Kate perched on the edge of the bed, staring out the window at the beauty of Custer State Park. The sun wouldn't set for another few hours. What was John Howard doing now? What was his next step? And how had he stayed ahead of them? "If the monuments went up last night, then the code had to be inserted into the security systems prior to last night."

"Prior to you putting in your trap doors?"

"Yes. I think so."

Donovan nodded in agreement. "Maybe forty-eight hours before, maybe longer."

"I could probably find the exact time, but it would take me a few hours—"

"No," Allison said. "I don't think we have time to do a full forensic analysis. And I'm not sure it matters. Even if we could backtrack to a time and use that to attempt to find the person or persons, what good would it do? We'd end up with our hands on a low-level hacker. Best case, we'd identify the goons who installed the monolith at Mount Rushmore. I seriously doubt John Howard personally did the coding or the installation."

Kate nodded in agreement. "Howard didn't strike me as the kind of guy who liked to do manual labor. He does, however, like to hire things out to the best in the business. In this case, I'm not certain who that is."

"I'm wondering if he's even been on site yet." Donovan leaned his head back and stared at the ceiling. "We know the facial recognition at Mount Rushmore hasn't tagged him, but does that mean anything? If he could hack in and loop the security cameras, couldn't he also loop the facial recognition system?"

"Harder to do. Most places routinely turn that portion of the program off when the facility is closed. Those programs aren't cheap to run. We got lucky that the director of Mount Rushmore opted to keep his on. He probably did so only because it's a holiday and a high traffic weekend."

"But it didn't help us?" Allison asked.

"No. The facial recognition cameras were designed to monitor people who came in and left the facility via guest or employee entrances and exits. Additional security cameras point directly at the monument itself to catch anyone who might want to leave graffiti."

Allison lay back on the bed. "Whoever installed the Mount Rushmore monolith must have accessed from a back road and stayed between the actual monument and the visitor center."

"It could have happened that way," Kate said, warming to the idea. "In fact, it probably did. There's no digital recording at all of that specific area."

"What was your assessment of the park director, Allison?" Donovan's gaze jumped from Allison to Kate and back again. "Neither of us found him to be particularly helpful, but in your opinion, could he be compromised?"

"Clarence Moss didn't strike me as particularly corrupt. Of course, we only spoke with him for a moment, and we weren't forthcoming in any way. The presence of the software, plus the fact that he kept it running overnight, seems to indicate he runs a pretty tight ship—"

"Doesn't mean he can be trusted. There are two possibilities here. He's compromised. He's not compromised. It's hard to assign a motive to the man's actions without knowing more about him. He could be simply covering his backside in case anything happens given the amount of unrest across the country right now." Donovan directed the next question at Kate. "Have you been able to do a deep dive into his background?"

"I have. Nothing jumped out. There was a problem with back alimony awarded at his divorce proceedings two years ago. The amount he was behind totaled a little over eight thousand dollars. All of it has been paid in the last year, and he's remained current since he accepted the position at Rushmore."

"Did he make up the back payments in one lump sum?" Donovan asked.

"Nope. He made up the deficit in regular payments. No big deposits or withdrawals from any of his accounts. He's had no major purchases and drives a three year old Ford—middle of the line. There were three parking tickets—2014, 2018, 2019. No other interaction with law enforcement."

"How do you know all that without even looking at your notes?" Donovan asked.

"Eidetic memory," Kate and Allison replied at the same time, then high-fived one another.

"Comes in handy sometimes," Kate admitted.

Allison beamed at her. "My partner has skills."

Seeing Donovan's look of mock despair, she quickly added, "Both of my partners do."

"I'm not ready to loop Moss in on what we think is happening," Donovan admitted, growing somber again. "But we could feel him out tomorrow. He wasn't interested in talking about the monolith today, but we could put some pressure on him. Get a reaction. Decide from there."

"That's fine," Allison said.

Allison and Kate had done a full analysis of park staff and employees weeks earlier, when their suspicions had first settled on Mount Rushmore. Kate honestly didn't think Clarence Moss was a member of the AT. In addition, she felt like Donovan and Allison had more experience on this type of active op, so she would defer to their decisions. If they had a question about being undercover or about the intricacies of coding, those were her domains.

Donovan went back to ticking facts off his fingers. "Security system breached, monoliths installed, warnings given. Feels like it's building up to something."

"None of this stuff is cheap," Allison said. "Ordering a monolith with a message? Ordering two of them? Then paying a crew to slip it into place in the middle of the night? How much money does Howard have?"

"A lot." Kate had often wondered the same thing. "I hacked into a few of his accounts undetected. It would be safe to assume he has several million at his disposal. But that's not the real question. The real question is how much money does Stella Gonzalez have? She's funding these operations. I'm sure of it."

"You never peeked into her finances?" Donovan asked.

"I tried, but it's as if she's buried her gold bars in a box in the backyard. Every search came up completely empty. Every inroad turned into a dead-end."

Allison stood and paced the room. "You're sure the money comes from her?"

"Yes. John would design the operational plans and present them to Stella. When she approved them, the money would appear in his accounts."

"And you couldn't trace where it came from?"

"No. It wasn't simply that the money bounced through several locations before landing in John's account. A couple of times I traced it back to the source, only to find that the source didn't and had never existed."

"How is that possible?"

"It's not."

Donovan had been quiet during this exchange. "We can't let ourselves be distracted by questions of how."

"Distracted?" Allison turned on him, her shoulders stiffened, her hands clenched at her sides. "Distracted? If we don't know where the funds are coming from, then we're merely playing whack-a-mole. We stop the AT this time only to have it pop up somewhere else in a week or a month."

"That's not what I'm saying."

Donovan waited, and Allison finally slumped back onto the bed.

Clearing his throat, he tried again. "We need to stop the AT now. Stop it permanently. And I think we can do it. What you two have done is amazing. You might not realize it, but you outsmarted the Agency's computer."

Allison shook her head, but her expression of frustration had melted away, replaced with focus and intensity. This was personal for Allison. Kate understood that, and she was sure that Donovan did as well. But it was personal for her in a different way, and she wasn't sure than anyone could quite grasp the full weight of that. She'd lived in Howard's lair, worked under his too intense gaze, worried every day that she would be found out and killed. Had she and Allison outsmarted the Agency's computer? Maybe. But maybe that was because they had more skin in the game.

She motioned for Donovan to continue.

"No one else picked this place, but you've convinced me. The existence of the monoliths along with the ciphers indicate that the AT is responsible, that they are planning something, and that it will probably take place tomorrow. The Task Force's program agreed with your prediction of July 4th. It differed in location—chose larger sites that would yield more casualties. Your conclusion that this would be a major message on a symbolic target feels spot on."

Kate felt both better and worse at those words. They mirrored her thinking exactly, and that was assuring. But it also meant that her worst nightmare was about to play out. People would be injured. John Howard might slip out of the vicinity without their catching him. She might never have her chance for revenge.

Was that what she wanted? Revenge? Or simply the assurance that his reign of terror was over?

"John Howard has spent a lot of money on the buildup to the big show. He's not walking away now. I don't think he could even if he wanted to."

"Do you think they're here, in Custer?" Allison asked.

Kate nodded. She wasn't afraid of John or Stella, not exactly. But the old sense of dread rose up. The entire time she'd been undercover, she'd felt that a clock was ticking, a clock that would signal her end. Maybe she had come to terms with the scars left by those two years spent undercover. Maybe not. Either way, the dread was back.

"I do," Kate said. "They'll be close, bounce off the local networks, show themselves at the optimum moment."

"But will it be at Crazy Horse or Mount Rushmore?" Allison walked to the glass door that opened out on the balcony and provided a view of the Black Hills. She stared intensely, as if she could see John and Stella and the entire AT crew.

"He'll hit both places," Donovan said. "A primary site and a backup site."

"What's our next step?" Kate asked.

Donovan glanced at the Faraday cage, then back at Kate. "I want you to write a program that monitors local cell tower activity. Search for signals that bounce from one tower to another. I think it's why we're not intercepting anything. They don't stay connected to any one tower long enough to trip our surveillance."

"He has the best programmers in the country. At least he did. What you're describing is entirely possible."

"While you're doing that, I'm going to track the monoliths."

"How? Where?"

Donovan nodded toward the Faraday cage.

Allison started laughing, and Kate said, "I should have brought bigger panels."

Allison looked relieved that they were doing something. "Where do you want me, boss?"

"I'm not the boss," Donovan muttered, but a smile tugged at the corners of his mouth. "I want you to go over to the park office and speak with the rangers. Someone has seen something. They just don't realize they've seen it."

"And you think they'll talk to me? I don't have my agency creds."

"You're persuasive."

"When I want to be."

"Which is all the time."

Kate loved the banter between her two teammates. It didn't make her feel lonely. It made her feel as if she were finally working in a normal environment—one where there was zero chance your boss would turn and fire a bullet through your head for some perceived injustice.

Donovan stood and stretched, his fingers just brushing the room's ceiling. "Let's meet in the lodge's restaurant in two hours. We'll grab something to eat, then reconnoiter the two sites together."

It was a good plan.

Kate only hoped that it was good enough to stop the AT before the attack began. She was certain that whatever chaos they had concocted would be far worse than anything they'd done before.

John Howard felt a strong inclination to break the neck of the woman standing in front of him. It would be so easy to do. So satisfying. He didn't give in to that urge because he suspected she might still prove useful. Instead, he waved her toward an empty park bench.

They sat together, watching tourists walk by.

He'd picked a spot where he knew there were no surveillance cameras. She'd requested a long lunch break from her job at the Mount Rushmore National Park office with the excuse that she had a doctor's appointment. They'd agreed to meet at the entrance to Custer State Park's wildlife loop, where they could blend in with the large holiday crowd. Business was hopping in the Black Hills.

The predicted holiday tourists had not cancelled their plans because of the chaos reigning over the airports, subways, and bus systems. Many who visited South Dakota drove there in their private vehicles which ranged from old station wagons that might not make the return trip to newer model SUVs, trucks, sedans, and crossovers. John could tell from the way they walked, from the slogans on their t-shirts, even from the firearms not-so-well concealed under their t-shirts that they considered themselves to be salt of the earth type folks. And maybe they were, but they, too, had become polluted with and dependent upon government-controlled technology. They stopped and checked phone messages instead of looking up at the scenery. They texted and facetimed and snapchatted. One young girl he'd passed was watching a Youtube video of prairie dogs instead of watching the critters right in front of her.

They refused to see that the device in their hands held them prisoner.

Did they even pay attention to the news?

Some of the phones were encased in QuantumGuard pouches. John knew all too well that if you created a problem, Silicon Valley would pump out a solution. As soon as this particular op was over, he would assign a programmer to find a way to hack through the pouches.

Or maybe, after the events of the next twenty-four hours, people would part ways with their idiot boxes. It was time for a dramatic shift in the way Americans operated on a day to day basis.

The appearance of the monoliths had succeeded in drawing even more people than were usually in attendance for *Independence Day ceremonies*. He loved that phrase. Those three words. They would, indeed, have their independence—though it would look nothing like what they saw in movies or read in books. This wasn't a spy novel after all. This was life.

He turned to the woman sitting beside him. "You're certain you saw Donovan and Quinn."

"Yes. Absolutely. Only the two, though. I didn't see the other lady."

He wasn't surprised. He rather suspected that Kate Jackson had run to ground and would remain off the radar for many years. She knew what he was capable of. Even if she had debriefed her superiors on the Cyber Task Force—which he was sure she had, Kate was always one to do her duty—her personality profile clearly showed that she was not the type to challenge him. She would fulfill her obligations, then quietly slip away and hope that he couldn't find her.

Allison Quinn, on the other hand, would chase him to the far corners of the Earth, and he respected that about her. In the end, it would be her downfall, and hopefully that moment would occur in this location, on this holiday, in the way he had planned it. She might be Stella's obsession, but he always enjoyed winning a solid match.

Donovan Steele would also respond aggressively to any perceived threat. Plus, he would be prudent to consider the relationship between Steele and Quinn. He might be able to twist that to his advantage.

Kate Jackson probably took a year's leave and rented a condo on some beach. Steele and Quinn were in the area and hot on his trail.

Two out of three wasn't bad.

He'd take it.

"What do you want me to do now?" The woman sitting beside him perched on the edge of the bench, eager to receive her next assignment.

It had been easy enough to comb the social media profiles of all park employees, find the ones who gravitated toward political discontent if not outright overthrow of the government. That, plus a sizable student loan that was taking a surprising chunk of her salary each month, had made her the perfect informant.

"Do?"

"You said they're a threat, said they needed to be stopped. As a park ranger, I have the authority to arrest. Wouldn't surprise me if those two are the ones who put those monoliths out. Trampling pristine forest to do so. Makes me sick."

"Yes, well. Please don't arrest them. We want to, err, follow them and find who they're working for."

"But aren't they dangerous?"

"No. Of course not. A little embezzlement. Some misappropriation of funds. We'll take care of it." He reached into his shirt pocket and pulled out a business card. "All I need you to do is call this number if you see them again."

"It's a different number from before."

"It rings through to a beeper."

"A beeper?"

"You don't have to leave a message. Just wait for the beep. Your number will be recorded, and I'll call you back."

The woman nodded, stood, resettled her hat against the westerly advancing sun. "People like those two are ruining this country. Makes me wish we didn't even have a government. All they do is suck money from the people, then keep it for themselves."

Her words fell like music to John's ears.

"The first half of our agreed payment has already been deposited into your account."

She nodded once, then felt the need to add, "I'm not doing this for the money, just to be clear."

"Of course you aren't."

"It'll help, sure. But I'm doing it because the American people —the ones who work five days a week, then go to their second job the other two—we're sick and tired of the way things are."

"Perhaps you will be instrumental in ushering in a new beginning."

She shrugged, as if that was too grandiose a thing to consider, then turned and walked away.

John Howard waited a few moments, then stood and walked over to Spencer, who was sitting two benches down.

"Did I keep her talking long enough?"

"Yup. Hacked into her phone, which then granted me access to her EV."

Ah, the *Internet of Things*. John despised it, but he had to admit that, at times, it was useful.

"Take care of her tonight."

"Not a problem. I can lock her brakes or disengage them completely. If I do so while she's cruising home at seventy miles an hour—"

John held up his hands. "I don't need the details, Spencer. Just take care of it. We wouldn't want her growing a conscience and reporting us to the authorities."

It would have been tempting to leave her in place, but there was very little useful information to be gained from it. He'd confirmed that Quinn and Steele were in the area. They would, no doubt, be at Rushmore the next day when the big event took place. He would see that they didn't walk away from the ensuing chaos.

Spencer slipped his laptop into his backpack and stood. He looked like a dozen other preppie, tech-immersed people enjoying a day in the great outdoors while remaining firmly connected to the World Wide Web. "Why did you give her the card?"

"As long as she thinks she's contributing to the cause, she won't be suspicious."

"I guess that makes sense."

"Yes, it does, Spencer. Which is why you want to always make sure you're contributing. Be very sure, each and every day, that you are useful to me."

Spencer gulped, causing his Adam's apple to bob. He was being paid exceedingly well and had little chance to spend the money. He was certainly planning an exit at some point in the future, but John would be surprised if he lived to implement it.

Spencer, Jasmine, and yes—even Stella wouldn't live to see the dawn on a new America. Nothing personal, but something he would see to out of an abundance of caution.

He'd be the last man standing in the AT organization.
It had always been lonely at that top.
He was used to it.
In fact, he rather enjoyed the solitude.

Chapter Eight

Allison met with the park rangers stationed across from their lodge and learned that while the monoliths were a source of interest and conversation, no one considered them a threat. There had been upwards of fifty such appearances in the U.S. since November 2020. Utah, California, Pennsylvania, Michigan, Colorado, even Texas had all played host to the unusual structures that usually disappeared as quickly, silently, and mysteriously as they had arrived.

One ranger she talked to actually floated the idea of aliens. Allison didn't have a firm opinion on the likelihood of life in the cosmos, but she was pretty sure aliens from Alpha Centauri hadn't placed a monolith near Crazy Horse and Mount Rushmore. No one travelled 40 trillion kilometers, then left a calling card with no return phone number.

The two hours spent at the ranger station, pretending to be a news correspondent, resulted in little actionable intelligence other than the fact that tribal authorities would be dealing with the monolith near Crazy Horse.

She shared all of this with Donovan and Kate at dinner. Both had spent the last two hours peering into monitors and appeared a little dazed to be out in the real world. Donovan had found three other monoliths that were similar in style, height and construction to the one at Mount Rushmore.

"All triangular with mirrored surfaces. Approximately ten to twelve feet tall. Appeared anonymously, and no one stepped up and claimed responsibility." Donovan pushed away the empty plate that had held spaghetti and drank an entire glass of water.

Allison often had the thought, watching him eat, of a powerful engine being refueled. The amount of carbs he'd just consumed should put him into a food coma, but Donovan would be locked, loaded, and ready to go.

"That's it?" Allison asked. "That's all you found out after two hours of cyber stalking?"

Donovan grinned at her. "The three similar monoliths originated from Australia, and they did not have a cipher. I traced the digital footprint of the original news coverage corresponding with each event. Each took me to a company called Earthwise Strategies in Perth. Got its start protesting the mining there and apparently took its message global."

Allison dropped her fork on top of her salad. "What message?"

"You're going to love this. *For the planet, we rise.* Seems to have started out legitimately enough, but a deeper dive into their finances and clients leaves little doubt that they're eco-terrorists."

Kate had been watching them, her mouth slightly ajar, her eyes widening.

"What?" Donovan asked.

"Have you heard of them?" Allison watched her friend closely, and she realized in that moment that Kate was, indeed, her friend. The fact surprised her a little. She'd never really taken the time to have gal-pals, but what she and Kate had been through the last few months had created a bond stronger than friendships that went back decades.

"I haven't heard the firm's name before." She blinked her eyes rapidly, then stole a furtive glance left and right. "But that slogan

—*For the planet, we rise*—I saw it on a notepad once in John's office."

"Okay." Donovan blew out a long breath, then tapped the table. "Confirmed connection. Or close enough."

"Yeah."

"Are you okay, Kate?"

"I think so." She shook her head, stared at her plate, then finally raised her gaze to Allison. "It just hit me that he could be here. He could be in this room, watching us at this very minute."

"He's not in this room. And even if he were, Donovan and I are here. We will collectively kick John Howard's ass. You know that. Right?"

"Yeah." Kate closed her eyes briefly, then opened them with an embarrassed smile. "I do know that. I'm struggling with the sudden realization that I am inside of one of my recurring nightmares."

Allison hadn't shared everything she'd learned about Kate with Donovan. Hadn't shared how deep the scars went from Kate's time undercover—the flashbacks and nightmares and paranoia. She hadn't felt it was her place, and now, looking at the two of them, she realized she didn't need to. She didn't make it a regular practice to talk to him about her recurring nightmare regarding the death of her father. When she woke shivering, he held her, brought her a glass of water, waited until her breathing returned to normal.

Donovan would have their backs without knowing their worst fears. She and Kate would have his. They were a team in the truest sense of the word.

An hour later, they stood at the pull-off, where they could see the monolith closest to the Crazy Horse Memorial. Given Kate's description, they'd decided that the Crazy Horse monolith would be easier to access. They couldn't articulate what they hoped to find, but the monoliths were the only clue they had at this point.

A good portion of the sky had turned a troubling black, as a brewing storm approached from the east. The ominous skies to the east contrasted dramatically with the western sky's setting sun —a tapestry of red, purple, and orange that shot out from the west, crossed the area where they stood, and bounced off the monolith, rendering it like a thing on fire. Every type of vehicle packed the parking area, but as darkness fell across the Black Hills, people lost interest. They corralled the kids, loaded everything in the car, cast one last look at the monolith, then drove away to eat, or put the kids to bed, or watch a movie in their hotel room.

"Star gazing's out," Donovan noted as a group of college kids loaded large telescopes into the back of a suburban and drove away.

"Weather changes fast in the Black Hills." Kate tugged a ball cap more tightly over her hair to keep it from blowing in her face. "We need to do this quickly."

Twenty minutes passed, and darkness blanketed the area, and they were alone. Allison led the way, followed by Kate, and Donovan held the last position. They each carried flashlights tinted red to protect their night vision. Making their way down the embankment, they moved carefully, quickly, silently. Allison thought the monolith seemed taller and more menacing when they stood next to it, staring up, considering the oddness of such a sleek, modern thing in the midst of the hills.

The wind had picked up even more, and now lightning occasionally split the sky.

Each took a side of the triangle, shining their light on the base, then working their way up. Kate knelt on the ground, brushed the dirt away from the plate that held the monolith in place. Someone had drilled holes and secured the thing with what looked like hurricane anchors. They shifted positions and repeated the analysis again, then once more. All three anchor plates had the smallest inscription, something Allison might not have seen if they hadn't just been discussing it.

ES

Earthwise Strategies.

They weren't able to see to the very top of the monolith, though Donovan's height afforded him a slightly better view. Allison shone her light as he reached up as far as his five-foot, eleven-inch frame allowed him to reach, running his fingers over the upper surface.

Nothing unusual there. No other clues. The rain pelted the ground in large, fat drops. Allison didn't mind getting wet, but she did not want to get caught in the bottom of a ravine with only a steep, muddy bank available for an exit.

They turned and started back toward the parking area, climbing up the bank carefully to keep from sliding back down. They'd made it a third of the way when they heard the rev of engines, and then they were bathed in bright white light and someone on a bullhorn said, "Turn around. Hands in the air."

The voice was slightly accented, almost musical.

Donovan nodded once, and the three turned—hands in the air, eyes looking down to avoid the glare of the lights.

Three men exited the group of jeeps. Allison could see now that there were half a dozen of the vehicles. Each sported a bar of spotlights mounted on top. All of the persons in the jeeps wore holsters and made no attempt to hide the fact. Sixteen men and women in all. As they slipped and slid down the slope, Allison could make out faces and patches on jackets and decals on the vehicles.

Tribal Police

Three against sixteen would have been a tough fight, and why bother? They had no beef with these people.

The rain had turned into a downpour, and the temperature had dropped fifteen, maybe twenty degrees. Allison's clothes stuck to her body like a second skin. The leader of the tribal police group, a tall man with prominent cheekbones, a strong nose, and long black hair, jerked his head toward the line of jeeps, and they were each walked toward separate vehicles.

Allison looked to Kate, who was watching Donovan. Kate raised her eyebrows, nodded ever so slightly back toward their van, but he shook his head once, and that was all it took. Donovan had the most experience as an operational leader. He'd weighed the pros and cons. It looked like rather than fight, they were meekly going along with whatever these people had planned.

At least for the moment.

The ride in the Rubicon jeeps was rocky. The hard top roofs did little to protect them from the storm that had unleashed itself upon the Black Hills owing mainly to the fact that the doors on the jeeps had been removed. They jostled up hills and down ravines, following no path that Kate could discern. She was surprised when the forest opened up and revealed a collection of metal buildings, twenty minutes from the site of the monolith and quite far back in the hills. There was another road—one of hard-packed dirt—leading in the opposite direction and away from the collection of buildings. Kate wondered how it would handle the deluge of rain. She didn't think they'd be leaving the way they came. Their escorts seemed unconcerned by the weather.

The tribal police officers ushered them into the middle building. The building to the left was the size of a barn and could easily house all of the vehicles. The one to the right? Supplies possibly. Or more monoliths? But she didn't actually believe that. Why would the Lakota Sioux tribe choose such a modern symbol to make a point? And the messages—*You are still being lied to* and *We will set you free*—those didn't sound Native American to her. Allison had been told the tribal police would be in charge of the monolith close to Crazy Horse. These people were simply doing their job.

One of the women nodded to a younger man and said, "Take

him into the interview room. We'll keep one of the women in the boss's office and the other in the break room."

"No," Donovan said.

Everyone turned to stare at him, including Kate and Allison.

"We do this together."

The officer's expression didn't betray any surprise, but her eyes—almond-shaped, dark brown, and unruffled—assessed him for a full minute before she nodded once and said, "Fine. Interview room's going to be crowded, though."

As they turned to follow their guide to the back room, a tall, athletic man walked in. His hair—thick, straight, black and tinged with gray—was pulled back with a beaded band and fell to his mid-back. He was older than the man who had led the group of officers in the jeeps, but they looked so much alike that Kate suspected there was a family connection.

"My office will be fine, Talia. And Leo, bring us four cups of coffee."

"Sure thing, Chief." Leo didn't question his boss or betray his feelings about that order.

Kate was quickly coming to the conclusion that these people kept their thoughts and reactions well hidden. She also took it as a good sign that no one had slapped handcuffs on them.

Talia added an extra chair to the two already in the chief's office for visitors. The older man took a seat behind the desk, though his posture remained ramrod straight. He waited for them to be seated, and then waited a little longer. Finally, he asked, "Do you know why we have detained you?"

"You think we have something to do with the monolith," Allison said.

"Do you?"

"Not in the way you think."

"What does that mean?"

"That we're on your side."

"You understand our side?"

"You know we didn't do it, or you would have already cuffed

us and read us our rights. Which begs the question.... How do you know it wasn't us?"

Kate wasn't sure why Allison was taking such an aggressive tactic. Maybe because they were all painfully aware that the clock was ticking. John Howard had set his plan in motion. They needed to be doing their jobs, not sitting in a tribal office drinking coffee.

The man sitting on the other side of the desk surprised her by standing and reaching across to Allison to shake her hand, then Kate's, and finally Donovan's. As he did so, he said, "My name's Tanner Red Cloud Larson. I'm the Chief of Tribal Police in this portion of the Black Hills."

Kate nearly fell out of her chair when Donovan said, "Donovan Steele. Pleased to meet you. These are my partners Allison Quinn and Katelyn Ballou. How far does your territory extend?"

She looked to Allison, who was obviously biting back some retort. No use arguing about it now, though. For a reason she didn't yet understand, Donovan was being completely honest with this man, even to the point of revealing their real identities.

"The jurisdictional lines are a bit of a quagmire in the Black Hills," Larson said. "My office is responsible for the area from Hill City to Custer, not the towns themselves, which are covered by local police, but the unincorporated areas. Who do you work for?"

"Joint Cyber Task Force—a coalition between the FBI and Homeland Security."

"Do you have ID?"

"Not to prove what I've just told you. In fact, our IDs are aliases." Donovan tossed a look at Allison.

Kate thought her friend looked as if she were ready to come unglued, but there was something about Donovan's approach that was starting to make sense to Kate. She'd read up on tribal police while doing her research.

They had full authority to arrest and detain tribal members.

Non-native individuals could be detained, but in most cases had to be handed over to state or federal authorities. There were sometimes agreements in place between tribal authorities and local, state, or federal agencies—but that wasn't always the case. The Lakota Sioux Tribal Police in the Custer area of South Dakota might very well prove to be an ally that they could use to their advantage against the AT.

Allison clearly had not reached the same conclusion. "Since my partner is being so forthcoming, let me add that we don't have time for this." Allison rose, but as she did, Leo walked in, balancing four cups of coffee on a tray. When Donovan reached for his, Allison sank back into her chair with a frustrated sigh.

Leo placed the tray on the desk and left. Larson handed out the cups, pushing the tray with sugar and cream to their side of the desk in case anyone wanted some. No one did.

Donovan took a gulp of his coffee and grimaced. "Allison's right. We don't have a lot of time, which is why I'm being straight with you. Obviously, you have some form of surveillance since we'd been at the monolith less than twenty minutes when you arrived."

Tanner smiled and sat back, ignoring his cup of coffee. "Drones and some game cameras. Nothing fancy. No access to satellites like your organizations have."

"Do you have footage of the people who installed the monolith?"

"We do."

"That's how you knew it wasn't us." Donovan finished his coffee and set the cup on the tray. "That's why you haven't formally detained us."

Kate felt like a rookie agent playing catch up.

"You're not local—obviously." Larson steepled his fingers together. "No one would have gone into that ravine with a storm from the east bearing down. And you certainly are not in league with the people who left the monolith. They were better equipped."

"Helicopters?"

"Yup."

"Team of men?"

"Four, plus the pilot."

"How quickly was it installed?"

"From the moment the copter set down until it lifted off, fourteen minutes. By the time our officers arrived on scene, there was nothing left except a faint mark in the grass where the copter had been."

"Did you share this with the local authorities?" Allison asked.

Larson reached for his coffee now, his eyes on Allison, assessing her, deciding exactly how much he was willing to share. Finally, he shrugged and said, "They didn't ask."

"Ah." Allison sat back. "Can we see the video?"

Larson grinned. "Going kinda fast for a first date."

"This isn't a joke." Allison jumped up and paced the length of the office, reminding Kate of a tiger in a cage.

"Are you aware there's a second monolith at Mount Rushmore?" Kate asked.

"We are, though that is not in our jurisdiction."

"We need to see your tape, or drone footage, or camera video," Donovan said.

Larson rubbed a hand up his neck, then down the length of his face. Kate had always been a good judge of people. She definitely felt she could detect anyone working for John Howard. They had a certain arrogance that she hadn't encountered anywhere else. This guy wasn't that.

Which was why she sat forward. "Do you know what a cyber task force is?"

"Sounds rather self-explanatory."

"Have you been watching the news? From across the country?"

"Yes. Is this connected to that?"

"It is."

"What could monoliths have to do with cyber-attacks?"

"They're sending a message."

"Do you know who *they* are?"

"We do," Donovan said. "And we don't think it's the people you have on camera. Those would be hired hands. We're pursuing the people financing and implementing the attack. Still, your footage could still be useful. Find the people they hired, trace the money back to the persons responsible. It's all about building a case."

Allison stopped pacing and jumped back into the conversation. "It's also about stopping them before they do the next thing, which will be infinitely worse than sending a signal."

"Okay." Larson stood. "Follow me."

He led them to a room large enough to hold maybe a dozen people. "Doubles as a conference room and a place to hold daily briefings." He pulled out his radio and said something to Talia. She entered the room a few seconds later, carrying a laptop.

"Talia's better with the technology side of things," he explained.

Less than a minute after that, they were watching game camera video of a helicopter landing, four men exiting, then pulling a long object out.

"Once the game camera video is triggered, the device sends a message to the person on duty. They then deploy the drones."

The display at the front of the room split into three distinct images, sourced from two drones and the game camera.

Beginning to end, fourteen minutes.

And though they were in a hurry, though Kate could feel the countdown clock Allison was so mindful of, felt it as if she could hear the damn thing ticking loudly and defiantly in her ears... she wanted a moment to process what she'd seen.

In spite of the very clear urgency of the situation, Allison said, "Can we watch it again?"

Kate didn't need to watch it again.

She remembered everything, or nearly everything, that she saw. It was the nature of eidetic memory. There were drawbacks, though. Sometimes it took a while for her mind to pull together the significance of large amounts of information—like fourteen minutes of video from three different sources.

Allison put a thumb on what was bothering Kate. "Back up. Can you zoom in? There. On the base of the rotor. Can you clarify it?"

Kate had seen it, but it was Allison's instincts that caught the most significant detail. They all stared at the logo, barely discernible, unnoticeable unless you had a game camera and a drone and Talia.

ES

"It's them." Allison dropped into a chair and stared at the other four people in the room—Kate, Donovan, Chief Tanner Red Cloud Larson, and Talia. "Earthwise Strategies. They're working with the AT and they're here."

"Who is the AT?" Larson asked.

"Anarchists for Tomorrow." Donovan pulled his gaze from the screen to the tribal police chief.

"Hackers?"

"More than that. They enjoy taking their diabolical cyber plans into the real world. Their name pretty much says it all."

They spent the next fifteen minutes sharing intel with Larson, while Talia scribbled notes.

"One more question." Larson had been mostly silent as they recited the nature and urgency of their mission. "Why are you traveling under aliases? Are you worried someone in authority is working with the AT?"

"It's possible that someone on our task force has been compromised, or someone on the local police force, or a national park employee." Donovan blew out a sigh. "There are other reasons, as well."

He looked at Kate, who explained, "If we travel under our names, the monitoring systems will flag us. There's simply too much surveillance in our society to allow for any degree of anonymity. Whether it's an ID scanned at a visitor center or a license plate captured on a freeway scanner or a facial recognition system running in the background."

"The AT has infiltrated some of those systems?"

"Probably all of them," Kate said. "I worked undercover with them for several years. If it's in the cyberworld, the AT can hack it."

Larson studied her, and it might have been her imagination, but she felt as if there was a glint of understanding in his nod as he accepted that and moved on. "You can change your names but not your faces."

"In most, if not all, instances, we know how to avoid the cameras," Donovan assured him.

"Okay. Tell me how we can help. Though being perfectly transparent, we don't have facial recognition at the Crazy Horse Memorial. There's not much to hack into there. I find it puzzling that this group left two monoliths. Is the one on our side of things a mere distraction?"

This time, Donovan looked at Allison and Kate before spilling the truth. "We think there's going to be an attack at both Mount Rushmore and Crazy Horse."

"A cyber-attack? How would that even..."

"No," Allison said, her voice a low whisper, or perhaps it was the predecessor to a snarl. "Not a cyber-attack. Something much more physical, more violent, and substantially more deadly."

Kate's stomach plunged at hearing those words, though of course they didn't come as a surprise. The AT's penchant for violence was always something to be considered. Her awareness of the possibility of violence in this situation brushed against her conscience every hour. Whatever John Howard had planned for the next twenty-four hours, more likely than not it would end in someone's death. She understood, had always understood, the type of threat they'd faced. She'd seen the violence behind John

Howard's calm demeanor. And Stella Rodriguez? Stella was a psychopath with a thin veneer of civility.

She had experienced both things firsthand.

Her mind—her eidetic memory—insisted on retaining every single thing she'd witnessed while working undercover in Middle Earth. The senseless and brutal murder of Brett Lindstrom. The horrific details of every operation that she'd helped the AT to plan and execute so that she could get ever closer to the center of things. So that she could feed information back to the JCTF and Donovan and Allison. So that she could stop not just one attack, but every future attack.

How long did they have before John Howard struck again?

One hour?

Twelve?

Probably no more than twenty-four. She knew, with complete certainty, that there would be a price to pay if they attempted to stop him. But there would be a price to pay, regardless. John wouldn't hold back this time—not on his final big splash. His warning to the world. And Kate firmly believed that this would be the final showdown. Only one side would emerge. No more stalemates. No more "we'll get you next time."

This was it. And she was ready.

Chapter Nine

John Howard could barely pull his eyes away from the evening news. Both monoliths had made a big splash. Tourism was up twenty percent in the Black Hills, even as cyber-attacks continued across the nation.

Subways sat silently on their rails.

Rideshares remained nationalized, their use reserved for essential workers.

Cell phones continued to blow up. The delayed programming that Spencer had inserted into the communication sector performed as promised. He'd give the kid a raise if he wasn't certain that it was necessary to kill him.

Not yet, though. He needed the young man's skills for the grand finale in the Black Hills.

The motel John had chosen wasn't the worst in town, but it certainly wasn't the best. Quinn and Steele would be actively looking for him. They'd start their search at the finer establishments—resorts, Airbnbs, vacation homes. By the time they checked the low budget establishments, he'd be long gone. The fact that they'd arrived in the Voltaris X would also help to render them invisible. What kind of terrorist arrived in town in such an ostentatious automobile? No. They'd think that his sweet ride belonged to a middle-aged man in the throes of a midlife crisis. The JCTF would look right over it.

He'd rented four adjoining rooms on the southwest corner of the building.

The receptionist at the desk assumed they were one big, happy family. "Enjoy your stay in the Black Hills," she'd called after them. "It's a vacation you'll never forget."

John didn't think anyone would forget this Fourth of July celebration.

Moving from his room—the largest and the one on the end—into Jasmine's, he barked, "Talk to me about social media."

"The monoliths are trending in the top three spots on X," she announced with the tiniest bit of pride in her voice.

"Make it number one, Jasmine. Second and third place are for losers."

"Right. I get that, but..."

John had always found that it was more effective to lower his voice rather than raise it. Let Stella be the screamer of the group. He intimidated through raw power. There was absolutely no need to raise his voice. So he walked over to the round table where Jasmine was working and placed his fingertips next to her small wrist that was resting on an ergonomic wrist rest—the very best that money could buy!

"I've given you every resource, and I expect you to deliver. Hire more bots. Flood the social media platforms. I want the monoliths to trend at the top of all of major sites, and I want them to stay there."

"Of course." She stared at her laptop's monitor, even leaned forward a little, but her fingers had stopped tapping the keys.

She reminded John of a rabbit caught in the focused beam of a white light. He tapped the tabletop, then splayed out his hand. Significantly bigger and stronger than hers. He left it there long enough for her gaze to drift over to his fingers and then bounce back to her monitor.

"I'll circle back in twenty minutes."

He moved into the next room to check on Spencer. It was nearing midnight. Certainly enough time had passed for him to take care of their unresolved matter.

Spencer glanced up and knew immediately why his boss was there. "All taken care of, and I confirmed it by tapping into the police scanner frequency. One deceased female on US-385. Seems the brakes on her EV went out at the same time that the accelerator stuck. Our park ranger won't be experiencing a change of heart. No more loose ends."

John knew that wasn't quite true. There might be loose ends within his organization, personnel that still needed to be addressed from their flight out of Wyoming. He'd put Spencer to work on that in the next few hours. Tomorrow was going to be busy, and after that.... Well, after that, Spencer wouldn't be around to help him anymore.

Having saved the best for last, he walked into Stella's room. He wasn't surprised to find no lights on and her sitting next to the window. Stella tended to sulk. From the light spilling through the doorway of Spencer's room, he could make out the glass in her hand—a little bit of ice, a small splash of dark amber liquid. Through a small gap in the curtains, a sliver of streetlight struck the bottle that sat on the table in front of her, made a little prism of color on the tabletop.

"I know you think I drink too much, John." She jostled the ice, then took another sip. Her long, deadly nails shimmered with their black, deadly polish. "In my opinion, you don't drink enough. You think I'm becoming a lost cause, but let me remind you... *not all those who wander are lost.*"

"Seriously, Stella? Another Tolkien quote?"

"What's wrong with Tolkien?"

Though it was the last thing he wanted to do, he took a seat at her table. "Your obsession with him strikes me as pathetic. And don't think I'm unaware of your meddling. Sending Quinn those messages? Foolish. And stupid!" He'd meant to confront her about it back at their homebase, but then their homebase had blown up—literally.

"Let me have my fun, John." She tipped the bottle toward the glass, rattled the cubes, poured, but somehow refrained from taking another drink. "You're young. I know you don't think you are, and yes, I realize you've been through a terrible loss."

"Move on to your point, Stella." His voice was a snarl, a barely concealed threat.

"I've been living with my loss for nearly thirty years. Imagine that. Imagine your entire life ruined by one person. By Arthur Quinn. Frodo, was his username, if you can believe that." Now she did reach for the glass and take a satisfying sip. "I began to build my empire before people even realized technology was something that would entice them, ensnare them. And Arthur, Frodo, ruined it all."

She stared into her drink, sipped it calmly, slowly, then, quick as a snake could strike, she hurled the tumbler across the room. The glass made a terrific sound as it hit the wall, smashing, sliding to the floor, leaving a debris field of scotch and ice and glass.

John sighed. He wanted to strangle this woman. She'd been a thorn in his side for too long. Yes, her money had been useful. It still was, but a man could only tolerate so much.

He did not place his hands around her neck.

Yet.

Instead, he leaned forward. "You want Allison Quinn? You want to satisfy this need for retribution? Then pull yourself together, Stella. Because this behavior will not cut it. We have less than twenty-four hours until the biggest attack of either of our careers. Now is not the time to lose your composure."

She cocked her head, took in the full measure of him, then flicked a wrist toward the shattered glass. "Everyone has to let off steam, John. Even you."

He didn't answer.

"You choose to kill someone when the pressure becomes too much. I throw a glass. Whose choice is more disruptive?"

"Depends who I decide to kill."

"Indeed."

The one thing he had to admire about Stella was the fact that she did not intimidate easily. He supposed her unflappable demeanor came from having so much money. She watched him with a calm, almost bored expression.

"How did you make your money, Stella? If Arthur Quinn foiled your cyber plans, how did you get to where you are today?"

"That's a long story. One that you would find quite boring." She pulled another glass toward her.

He hadn't noticed she had three more of the tumblers sitting there. Hopefully, she wasn't planning on shattering each one after drinking out of it. This motel was cheap, but the repeated sound of breaking glass might alert the guests next door. Guests who might call the overnight clerk, who might call the police.

He needed to placate her for a few more hours.

The final payment transfer hadn't been made yet, wouldn't be made until the RPGs had been used. He'd already directed Spencer to intercept that payment which was coming from Stella and redirect it to his own offshore accounts. After all, a man had to eat, and he didn't plan on leaving his country poor. No. He would leave it immeasurably wealthier than his great-great-grandfather had ever imagined when he'd immigrated to the United States.

He reached for a glass, used the tongs to pull exactly three pieces of ice from the small bucket she'd set beside the glasses. Apparently, she'd planned out her night with great precision. He dropped the ice in his glass and poured a finger of the scotch. At least it was Macallan, priced at $60,000 a bottle. Was that what she'd been so intent on storing in her bag when they'd fled Wyoming? Seventy-two-year-old scotch?

"Explain it to me," he said. "Tell me your long story."

Stella's expression softened, and for a moment he could see the younger woman, the one who wasn't yet wrecked by bitterness and loneliness and liquor.

She seemed to hesitate, then narrated her story as if it were an expose she'd read in the paper. As if it hadn't broken her heart and ruined her future. She told him how close she'd grown to Arthur —virtually close at a time when America didn't yet have email. She'd thought that he was the one. That he was a true believer, like she was. That he cared for her.

The betrayal, when she'd discovered it, had been devastating. Learning that he actually worked for the U.S. government had destroyed her confidence in being able to read people. Arthur Quinn was working for a newly conceived cyber force. He was working to destroy the very kingdom she was building. The gall of that. The bitterness.

She'd continued with the ruse that they were soulmates.

Watched him.

Monitored every keystroke.

Tracked him.

And followed him to the Redwood forest of Northern California.

"I put a bullet in his head, but not before he'd shouted run to his daughter." She hadn't stayed around to find the child. She'd never considered that the young girl, that Allison Quinn, would grow up to be a Homeland Security agent, intent on capturing the person who had murdered her father. Determined to keep the World Wide Web safe. Obsessed with her mission nearly as much as Stella was obsessed with hers.

Stella tapped her fingernails against the table. "Promise me I can have Allison."

"She's yours. I have no need for her." John had been holding back, but now was the time to close the deal, to ensure that Stella would stay focused through the very end. He checked his watch. Less than nineteen hours before the fireworks started. Surely she could hold it together that long, given the right incentive.

He drained his glass, leaned forward, waited for her somewhat blurry gaze to lock on his. "She's here, you know."

"In South Dakota?"

"Yes. Here in Custer. She'll be at Mount Rushmore tomorrow. I guarantee it."

The unfocused gaze became piercing. Had she been faking her drunkenness? Was Stella trying to play him?

"I want her. I want to kill her—up close and personal."

John stood, straightened his suit jacket, and carefully chose his next words. "Help me finish this mission first, then yes. You can have her."

"You could have checked with us first. That's all I'm saying." Allison knew she sounded unreasonable. They were back in the van, having been deposited in the parking area by Larson's people.

"But you understand why I did it. I've dealt with people like Larson before. Did you notice the Semper Fi tattoo? He would have smelled bullshit and shut down."

"You weren't wrong, Donovan, but a heads-up would have been nice?"

Donovan tossed a grin back at Kate. "What do you think, Kate? Should I have asked for five minutes alone in the interview room so we could confer?"

"Considering that we would have been monitored that might not have worked as well as one would hope."

"Ha! See. I'm right."

"I am not getting in the middle of this."

"It's not a lover's spat. It's more a group dynamics thing." Allison smiled as she buckled her seat belt. "Ended well, though. I'll give you that. Larson and his crew sound all in."

"Yup. And we'll need the help." Donovan hadn't started the van yet.

They were parked at the far end of the lot, since that had been the only spot open at sunset when they'd first arrived to see the monolith. There dim parking lamps, with *night friendly skies* stickers pasted on every pole, provided enough light to see each other by, or at least see the shadow of each other. Donovan turned in his seat and studied both Allison and Kate.

"We have a decision to make. Do we alert Kendra Thomas? Or Reid Clark? Or even Kenneth Langston?"

Allison felt the weight of that decision sitting between them —a large, heavy, palpable thing. "Kate, what is the likelihood that the AT has hacked into our internal system?"

"One hundred percent. The question isn't *if* they're in. The question is how deep they've been able to tunnel."

"If we report this, they'll know that we're on to them. They'll go to their alternate site."

"I agree," Donovan said. "But there's only three of us."

"Plus the Lakota Sioux Nation," Kate said. "At least the local part."

"As long as we all understand what is at risk here, and I don't only mean the lives of those who might die if we're not able to stop this attack. That would not be our fault. Any death and destruction will be the AT's fault, but we will be blamed. Every decision we make going forward will be judged by our superiors."

Kate nodded in agreement. "Plus every decision we've made that led to this moment."

"Everything is always scrutinized." Allison threw up her hands. "I understand what you're saying, but we can't plan a mission based on how the report will read."

She understood that wasn't the worst of it. Kate finally put into words the thing that had been niggling at Allison. The thing that kept her from eating more than a few bites, robbed her of sleep, put a bitter taste in each and every day.

"I can live with being blamed," Kate said. "It's the nature of our job for every operation to be analyzed, for our decisions to be subject to intense scrutiny. What I can't live with—the thing that keeps me awake when I should rest—is the thought of John Howard and the AT slipping through our fingers again. Look at what Allison endured in the Grand Canyon, what you both went through aboard the *Harmony of Dreams*."

"Still have the scars to prove it," Donovan muttered.

Kate was sitting in the back seat but looking out the front windshield. Staring into the darkness, but seeing the enemy. "Consider what our country is going through right now. The AT doesn't get to keep doing this. I know John Howard pretty well, and I guarantee you he's hoping we'll second guess ourselves, hesitate while we force the decision on someone higher up the chain, take the safer route."

Silence filled the van, and it seemed to Allison that with it came a measure of peace. Donovan had been right to bring this up, to force them to pause for a moment and consider the path they were about to sprint down, weapons raised, objective in their sight. Allison performed exceedingly well in such critical points of an operation. Her instinct was nearly always spot-on. Nearly. But she wasn't so good at pausing, considering her course, and committing to it on a conscious level.

"If and when we have irrefutable confirmation of him being here, then we reconsider calling the boss," Kate said.

Allison nodded. "I can live with that."

"We're agreed then," Donovan said. "Do what works. Choose the path that is most likely to resolve this issue, our careers be damned. Do not send it up the chain. Do not hesitate."

And then he added what he knew would make both Allison and Kate smile. "Game on."

"Game on," Kate echoed.

"Agreed," Allison said. Then she did something that she had rarely done in her life. Maybe with Aunt Polly. But had there been anyone else that she'd cared for as much as she cared for the two people in this van? She unbuckled, half-crawled into the back seat and gave Kate a long hug, then she kissed Donovan's cheek, dropped back into her seat, re-buckled, and said, "Let's do this. Game on."

The storm had abated, though the roads were still wet as they drove toward Mount Rushmore. Once there, they parked on an adjacent road rather than drive into the parking area, then they jogged toward the sight of the monolith. Kate led the way, since her amazing recall could be counted on to remember every spot under camera surveillance.

They accessed the Presidential Trail from the woods. It was now close to one in the morning. The clouds were moving west, and the moon intermittently broke through. It was during one of those brief flashes of light that they clearly saw four men climbing the rocky slope toward the monolith.

They'd stepped off the trails and into the woods for a better look. Donovan nudged Kate, who nudged Allison, and then Donovan nodded back toward the trail. When they were certain they were out of earshot, he whispered, "Tell me how you want to handle this."

"John Howard thinks those monoliths will be gone tomorrow," Kate said. "We know, for a fact, that won't happen at the one near Crazy Horse."

"Larson will be watching it like an eagle."

"And we told him to intercept and detain."

"So, we do the same," Allison said. "It'll come as a real shock to John, Stella, and the AT when they show up tomorrow and find both monoliths still in place."

Donovan gave them a thumbs up in agreement. "It'll be even better if he doesn't know what's happened—whether his cohorts got cold feet or got caught."

"There's a good chance we'll put him off his game," Kate said. "I'm in."

"There's four of them." Allison jerked a thumb back in the direction of the monolith. "Three of us. How do you want to do this?"

Donovan looked up and into the darkness, though he couldn't really see much of anything from where they were. "Four guys, but only three paths of escape leading away from the monolith. Allison, take the east side. Kate, take the south. I'll go west. Hold off until you hear my signal."

"Which is?" Kate asked.

Instead of answering, Donovan let out a hoot that sounded remarkably like an owl. Allison almost laughed at the look of admiration on Kate's face.

"We'll whistle when we're in place," Allison said.

"You've learned how to whistle?"

"I had some down time."

"Uh-huh."

"Kate?"

"Yeah. I can whistle."

And then they separated, but Allison didn't feel she was in this alone. It wasn't at all like the Grand Canyon, or even the cruise ship—after Donovan had been shot. This time, she had a team. This time, John Howard was the one who was going to be playing catch-up.

She was in position within fifteen minutes. The four men who were trekking toward the monolith were plainly not used to the rugged terrain. They also weren't expecting company, because they weren't making any attempt to mask their noise. Sounded like bears crashing through the woods.

Alison heard Donovan's signal, then Kate's. She replied in return and felt a little proud that she had learned how to whistle. It wasn't as easy as one might think.

The men had now reached the monolith and were pulling out tools from their backpacks. They'd obviously done this before.

As one, Donovan, Kate and Allison stepped out of the woods, weapons raised, forming a semi-circle and effectively denying them any escape route unless they planned to climb up the granite face to the presidential memorial.

Allison barked, "Stay where you are and put your hands in the air."

Four men turned—a big guy, one with a beard, another tall and skinny, and finally a guy who didn't look of legal age to buy a beer. It had always helped her to name her potential targets—Big, Beard, Skinny and Babyface. All stood there, eyes wide, mouths open in surprise. Big was the first to recover. He darted in Donovan's direction, which was a mistake. Donovan holstered his weapon and tackled him like the guy was on the four yard line and threatening to score. He didn't. He went down with a "whoof."

As Allison moved closer to the young man on her side, Donovan pulled zip ties from his pocket and secured the big guy. The man in front of Allison, Babyface, looked to be maybe nineteen years old, with the soft physique and pale complexion of someone who spent most of his time on-line.

"I wouldn't try running," Allison said.

He held his hands in front of him, showing he was unarmed, and backed up until he came in contact with the monolith. Letting out a squeal, he covered his head, as if Allison had put the monolith there for the single purpose of intimidating him.

Kate's guy—Skinny—was trying to climb up the granite rock face. Kate raised her weapon, took her time aiming, and hit a rock one foot above and to the right of the guy. Rock spewed, and the climber fell backwards. He lay there, staring up at the sky. As Kate secured him, he repeatedly whined, "You could have hit me—with a bullet!"

But where was the fourth guy? Where was Beard?

She turned and saw that he was attempting to run past Donovan. Bad idea. The hit to the first guy looked gentle compared to what Donovan did now. He went in low and fast. Allison heard the collision from where she stood. Donovan literally lifted the guy off the ground when he tackled him, throwing him back and down.

Beard lay on the ground, unmoving.

"Did you kill him?" Kate asked.

"Nah. Knocked the breath out of him. He'll live." Donovan rolled the guy over, secured the man's hands, then lifted him to his feet. His head lolled a bit to the right and left, and his legs seemed incapable of carrying him. Donovan stepped closer, hissed something in his ear, and the guy found his feet.

They quickly lined up all four men under a stand of pine

trees. No use staying out in the open since anyone could be operating a drone, or be watching via hacked satellite coverage.

"Who are you working for?" Allison asked.

"Screw you." This from Big, who seemed to have recovered from his hit. He attempted to puff out his chest, which apparently caused his shoulder to hurt. He'd probably fallen on it when Donovan had tackled him. Grimacing, he added, "We don't have to tell you anything."

"You don't? Because from where I'm standing, looks like you've trespassed on federally protected land."

"So. Sue me."

"Oh, you will appear in a court of law. Trust me on that." Allison moved in front of Big, who was trying to appear brave in front of his cohorts. But she saw the slight tremor in his jawline, the way his gaze jumped from spot to spot, noted his shallow breathing. "I'll bet my friend knows the exact laws you're violating."

Kate joined her in front of the guy. "Title 18, U.S. Code, Section 1361. Destruction of property. Fines up to $250,000, imprisonment up to 10 years, and that's for any federal monument. Mount Rushmore is special. I suspect the prosecution will insist on restitution as well."

"We didn't even touch the memorial," Big insisted.

"Yeah. And we want our lawyer." This from Babyface—the guy who had bumped into the monolith and jumped as if he'd been bit.

Allison jerked toward him, and he flinched, letting out a squeal.

"Careful now," Donovan said. "You don't want to give him a heart attack before he tells us who he works for."

"We don't know who we work for," Big said. He shuffled from one foot to the other, shook his head, and accepted their current situation. "We were paid with bitcoin. No names. No contact at all."

"You had to receive the specifications and instructions regarding the message that was engraved on the monolith."

"We don't build them, dude. Do we look like the kind of people who could build something like that?" He looked over at the monolith, now gleaming in the moonlight. Looked at it, and for a moment seemed mesmerized. "We just take them where we're told."

"Told by whom?" Kate asked.

"By the buyer."

"Shut up, Clint."

This time, Allison did backhand Babyface. He cried out and tried to sink his head between his shoulders like a turtle.

Clint had given up, though. Clint was the brains of this group, which wasn't saying a lot.

Donovan pulled the guy forward, dusted him off, then stepped closer. "What were your orders?"

"Have it in place before the 3rd. Leave it thirty-six hours. Have it removed before sunrise on July 4th." He sighed heavily, as if this entire sequence of events had exhausted him. "Kind of a short turnaround, if you know what I mean. What's the point of spending all that money if the thing is only going to sit there less than two days?"

"Sometimes less is more, Clint. Where's your helicopter?"

"They only provided it for delivery. Removal details were left up to us."

"And you installed the other monolith as well?"

"Yeah."

They collected the men's cellular devices and pocketed them all in case John Howard had installed a remote tracker on them. Destroying them would look suspicious, as would leaving them buried somewhere near the monolith. Howard expected the guys to retrieve the monolith, then move on to the next monolith. The phones, for now, would stay in the vicinity of the four blockheads in their custody.

"Where do we take these guys?" Kate asked.

"I'd rather not go to the local police." Allison crossed her arms. "Once their apprehension is made public, John will run to ground."

"We could take them to Larson." Donovan waited for both Kate's and Allison's reaction.

Tanner Red Cloud Larson had explained that they had the authority to arrest and temporarily detain anyone committing a crime on tribal land.

"This isn't part of Larson's territory," Kate pointed out.

"True," Donovan said. "But these guys were headed to pick up the Crazy Horse monolith next."

They had been speaking in low voices, but now Donovan raised his voice and addressed Clint. "Is that right, Clint? Were you headed to get the Crazy Horse monolith after this one?"

"Yeah, man. It was going to be a long night."

"Well, your night just got even longer, my friend."

Seeing their leader cave had taken the fight out of the other three guys. These four were not terrorists. They weren't even protestors. They were four guys looking to make a buck, not understanding what they were involved in, not caring to know the details.

Their transport vehicle was parked a quarter mile away. It would have been a difficult trek carrying a monolith, but maybe the object wasn't as heavy as it looked. Once they all arrived at the vehicle, Donovan fetched the key fob out of Clint's pocket, unlocked the door, opened it and prodded the men to get inside.

They all fit on the second bench seat, though it was tight. Better than letting them roll around in the cargo hold.

Stepping back from the van, Donovan asked, "What do you think?"

Kate frowned and shook her head at the same time—the equivalent of a double negative. "This thing is brand new. It can be tracked a dozen different ways."

"Okay." Donovan put his hands on his hips and studied the offending vehicle. It was a new model Dodge—still had that new car smell to it. Extra-long cargo bay. "If we leave it here, the AT will know something's up."

"Who's the AT?"

"Shut up, Clint." Allison's adrenaline was pumping. She could smell blood on the trail—metaphorically.

"How about this?" Donovan rubbed his hands together. "We drive this vehicle back to our van and load the guys into it. Allison and I will take them to Larson."

"And I'll drive their van to a back road near the Crazy Horse monolith."

"Park it there for at least..." Donovan ducked his head into the van where the men were waiting. "How long does this kind of job usually take, Clint?"

"Three hours, man."

"Three hours. Park close enough that you can hike back to the parking area where we were earlier. We'll pick you up, grab something to eat, then go back and move their vehicle."

"Any chance we could get some of that grub?" Beard asked.

"They'll feed you in jail," Allison said.

Donovan walked to the door of the van. Allison thought he must have looked larger-than-life, looming over the open door. She wouldn't have wanted to be in those men's shoes. They were just four guys who had stumbled across a way to make a buck and grabbed it. They'd done so with no idea what they were getting involved in or how deeply they would regret their association with the AT. It was pretty obvious they didn't even know who the Anarchists for Tomorrow were or their ideology or their plans for the next day.

"You have anything else to tell us, Clint?"

"Like what?"

"Like anything that might make our job easier. Anything you know you haven't shared."

"What's in it for me?" Clint's voice didn't sound arrogant. The man was defeated, plain as the slump of his shoulders. Instead of waiting for an answer, he said, "Stay off the trail."

"Those were your directions?"

"Yeah. Remove the monolith. Stay off the Presidential Trail. Access via a different direction. It's why we parked here."

"There may be hope for you yet, Clint." Donovan walked back to Allison and Kate. "Kate, we'll meet you at the highway pull-off. Allison and I will leave these guys with Larson and pick you up. We'll drive to the all night diner in Custer.

"Then go back and pick up their van, take it out of town and leave it." Allison practically bounced on the balls of her feet with energy and focus.

"It's a good plan," Kate agreed. "Let's do it."

Which is how they found themselves driving back toward Crazy Horse, the monolith, and the Lakota Sioux Tribal Police facility with four guys who'd been caught up in a plan much bigger than they could have imagined. The digital clock on the dash read two twenty-seven. The sun would be rising by five thirty, and they needed to be in place when it did.

The next eighteen hours would determine who won and lost, and possibly who lived and died.

Chapter Ten

John Howard woke without an alarm after his customary four hours of sleep. The cheap clock on the bedside table read twenty-seven minutes after five. Opening the drapes revealed a small tourist town and a dawn just breaking, promising a historic day.

How many people drinking their morning coffee had an inkling what was about to happen? He might be the only one. Not even the people who worked for him, or the woman he worked for, knew every aspect of the plan. The people whose mission it was to stop him were almost certainly clueless, at least as to the details and the severity. There was no way for them to know. Only he knew the details, and he certainly hadn't leaked them. He'd planned this alone, and in the end, he'd execute it alone. Certainly, the mercenaries he'd hired would play their part, as would Jasmine, Spencer, and Stella. But history would record John Howard as the author of today's events. He would be credited with freeing the American people.

Staggered attacks.

High visibility.

A biological weapon that guaranteed success.

He'd carefully executed every aspect of this mission. Sectioned off what each person knew so that no one who chose to betray him—like Kate Jackson, aka Katelyn Ballou—could shut down the project. That risk had been minimized since his crew was down to the two who'd better still be working in the attached rooms and Stella Gonzales, who no doubt would sleep in and wake with a raging hangover.

It was a momentous day indeed, but even so, it was best to follow his normal routines. Otherwise, what was the point of having them? Routines provided order in a chaotic world. They also served to clear his mind and sharpen his thinking. He commenced with his ritual of one hundred sit-ups and one hundred push-ups, though he'd forgotten to pack the bar that would secure to a doorway and allow him to complete fifty pull-ups.

No matter.

His blood was pumping. Since he'd passed the big 5-0, he'd embraced a renewed vigor for pushing his body to its limit. In the near future, he'd move his rebellion overseas. At that point, he'd have a gym installed in his villa by the sea. John had researched countries without formal extradition treaties with the U.S., but the list had been dismal. The Middle East, Africa, Asia, and Russia. None of those countries met his conditions for a life lived in exile—a word that didn't quite fit his situation. After all, he was a hero to the people of his country, and they would understand that one day.

He'd finally settled on a tiny island near Naples. Procida offered a slow pace and fewer crowds, while still providing adequate dining opportunities. He found it quaint that the Italian government considered itself to be a representative democratic republic. Obviously, they didn't quite understand the meaning behind those particular words. The Italian populace was as enslaved to their gadgets as the American people. He'd begin working on their freedom once he was settled into his villa.

Breakfast consisted of yogurt with a cup of strong black coffee, though he had to forgo his single boiled egg and toast.

There was only so much you could expect on the culinary spectrum from a small, cheap hotel room. He'd sent Jasmine out for the yogurt the day before. Once he'd eaten, he showered for two minutes exactly in water that was tepid at best. From his go-bag, he pulled out a clean, black t-shirt, then pulled on the black pants, black sports coat, and black shoes from the day before. He wouldn't pass for a tourist, but then he didn't plan on being seen until the last possible moment. Black clothing presented well on live video—authoritative, stylish.

The bedside clock read six fifteen. Time to check on the kids! Time to experience the day of America's independence in a whole new way. He could barely contain his excitement.

He didn't bother knocking on the adjoining door. After all, he'd paid for the room. He was surprised to see Jasmine and Spencer working at the same table, both leaning toward their screens and typing furiously. Their expression was not one of anticipatory glee.

"What's wrong?"

"The monoliths are still in place," Spencer said.

Perhaps he should have taken ten minutes of slow breathing with his phone's meditation app. John suddenly felt as if his brain might explode. Tamping down his rage, he counted to three and barked, "Explain."

"Explain what?" Jasmine didn't even bother to look up. "The monoliths are still standing. There's been live coverage from the sites since the sun came up."

"Why didn't you alert me?"

"We knocked on your door. You must have been taking a shower."

Jasmine was not giving John the respect that he deserved. That he demanded. He strode across the room, lifted her from the ragged desk chair, pushed her toward the wall, and held her there—several inches off the ground—with his right hand wrapped around her throat. Those morning exercises were really paying off. His own strength surprised him.

Her eyes refused to meet his, and her complexion had gone from flushed to waxy pale.

"I suggest you speak to me with a little more deference, Jasmine, or you won't live to sing *America the Beautiful* with the rest of the kiddies tonight."

"Right," she croaked.

"Right, what?"

"Right, Sir."

He almost rolled his eyes. "Better. Though honestly..." He released his grip, and she landed on wobbly legs with a thud. Straightening the wrinkled t-shirt she still wore from the day before, he added, "Sir isn't necessary. Mr. Howard would be fine."

"Mr. Howard, we have another problem."

Spencer looked as wasted as Jasmine. Did these two not understand this was the big day? They needed to be on their A game. John was beginning to wonder whether they had been the right two to bring along.

"Julio and Cloe have been trying to contact us through our secure channel."

"Those two?" Julio and Cloe were two of the lower level hackers—geniuses of course, but problematic in other respects. Julio had the irritating habit of repeating everything he said twice. Cloe believed their ultimate goal was to work in conjunction with governmental agencies. Young and immature. He'd had no choice but to leave them in Wyoming. "You're certain that's who it is?"

"Yes. They have the passcode which allows them to ping the server. Each operative was given a different passcode. It's definitely Julio and Cloe."

"Yikes."

"I haven't answered, but they're pinging at regular intervals. What would you like me to do?"

"Why are they still alive?"

John noticed Jasmine shoot a startled look his way. He turned on her with a fury as sharp and cold as the storm that had blown through the night before.

"Focus. On. Your. Job! Find out why those monoliths are still standing and what has happened to the idiots we hired to take them away."

She gulped visibly, her throat still red from where John's hand had been a few minutes earlier. "Right." She sat in her chair and began pecking at the keyboard.

John tilted his head toward the area outside. Spencer stood and led the way out of the motel room. What the motel lacked in amenities it made up for in location, positioned on a small rise with a good view of downtown Custer.

In a low voice, Spencer explained, "They started pinging the emergency number forty-five minutes ago."

"We got rid of that phone. Threw it out the window of the Voltaris X while driving over a hundred miles an hour."

"Right. Which destroyed the phone itself, but the number still exists. I don't know how Julio and Chloe survived the explosion or the resulting fire, but they are definitely the ones pinging the number, which I've been monitoring online."

"Could mean they're compromised."

"It could."

"No way to know." John sighed as if he were disappointed. He was disappointed. Those particular loose ends were supposed to be tied in a pleasant knot. Life was a challenge at times. "You loaded the kill program into their phones?"

"I did."

"Activate it." John turned away, but his gaze snagged on the Voltaris X—what a beautiful piece of machinery! It was a shame he couldn't take it with him to Italy. Or maybe he could. Though the expense would be prodigious, he could have the vehicle flown over, or put on a container ship—not that he trusted those fools with such an advanced piece of machinery. Still, there might be a way to transport it. People did transport cars all the time. When he'd worked in military intelligence—an oxymoron, if ever he'd heard one—he'd been attached to various embassies around the world. The government had regularly transported all of his family's belongings.

His family.

John's mind wanted to dwell on that, to take a moment to remember what had sent him down this path.

Later. He'd think about Lillian and Penelope later. He'd toast his little lost family from his villa in Procida. Not now. He envisioned putting their memories in a safe box within his mind and locking it. There! Mindfulness, like meditation, was actually quite amazing. His mind felt clear, light almost, and ready for what lay ahead.

The emancipation of America.

His chance to prove his patriotism.

His opportunity to provide a much needed course correction.

Kate checked her data twice. She knew it wasn't wrong, but she was having trouble processing the implications.

"What is it?" Allison asked. She sat slouched in the armchair next to the plate-glass window and had opened the drapes just enough to allow an inch of the morning light to peek through. "You stopped tapping on your keyboard and have been glaring at the screen for a good fifteen seconds. What's wrong?"

"Maybe we should get Donovan."

"He was in the shower ten minutes ago. For all I know, he's already sleeping like a baby. That's why I came over here. My intensity sometimes inhibits his sleep pattern." Allison threw her a smile. "But I knew you'd still be up."

"Okay. You should probably come and look at this."

Allison stood and walked over to the makeshift Faraday cage. She could see Kate's screen through the panels. "What am I looking at?"

"I wrote the program that Donovan suggested—to monitor local cell towers and see who was bouncing from tower to tower.

Mind you, there are only three towers in the area, so one wouldn't expect to see a lot of activity. I set the program to monitor and then we left."

"And now?"

Kate pointed to a flashing dot on the screen. "I got him."

Allison stared at the screen. "John Howard?"

"I think so." Kate's stomach burned with that admonition. They were so close now. He was literally a few miles away. "I mean, no one else would do this. And here's how I know it's John. The bounces aren't happening at random intervals, but they aren't exactly a regular pattern either."

"How can it be neither of those things?"

Kate brought up a pivot chart. "It's designed to look random. Say you need reliable, fast internet service, and so you create a program that will switch to the strongest signal—similar to what mobile network providers do."

"AT&T Air?"

"Sure. Most providers use the same performance model—Verizon, T-Mobile, all the big guys. They switch towers based on a variety of factors—signal strength, signal quality, tower loading balance, network optimization. It's a complicated formula, but once the programming is in place, it's also straightforward."

Kate pushed a couple of buttons on the screen. The pivot chart changed to a graph with two lines. She turned to check and make sure Allison was still watching. Her friend's eyes were focused on the screen.

"The blue line represents what the mobile service providers have done over the last twenty-four hours."

"And the red line?"

"The AT. John Howard. It has to be them. Look at this switch between towers." She pointed to a spot where the blue line remained horizontal, but the red line spiked, then fell lower. She tapped the keyboard, and the program switched to a graph. "All of those factors we talked about were acceptable when the red line switched. The mobile service providers didn't switch because there was no need to do so. The only reason for someone to do that is to hide their tracks. To keep from being traced. To keep from being caught."

She keyed in a few more commands, and the display split into four graphs. "Area service providers are shown in the bottom left. The AT bottom right. These bottom graphs show their activity. The top graphs coincide with access to cell towers. They're switching in what at a casual glance would appear to be a random way—the top right graph. It doesn't coincide with service providers—top left. And once charted, it occurs at an uneven, but regular interval."

"Like a randomized patrol."

"Exactly."

"Sophisticated."

"Very."

"John Howard."

"Yeah, and the only person I know who can write code that sophisticated is Spencer Parsons." She fidgeted with her thumb nail. "We know there was a raid on their last location and that John and Stella were not caught. We know they escaped, but we don't know who escaped with them. I think John and Stella left with at least one programmer, maybe two."

"Okay. Do you have a location on the data source?"

Kate nodded, searched her friend's eyes, then turned toward the monitor and hit a single key. A google map appeared with a single dot. Above the dot were the words *The Rusty Spur Inn*.

"Let's go check it out."

"Without Donovan?"

A silence filled the room, and Allison smiled. "I can hear him snoring through the walls. Let him catch a few Z's. We'll do one drive by."

"We won't intervene?"

"Not yet." Allison pulled her service revolver out of its holster, checked it, and replaced it in the holster.

"Why are you checking your piece?"

"To be safe. You know what they say in DHS school—always be safe."

"No one said that to me, except maybe my mother when I was nineteen and attending college."

"I heard it somewhere." Allison reached for the cotton shirt she wore over her t-shirt, shrugged into it, and picked up the keys to the clunker Volkswagen van they would use for surveillance. "Ready?"

"Sure. But on the way back, I want coffee—real coffee. Espresso strength."

Allison threw an arm around her shoulders. "With a donut. We're going to need sugar and caffeine. Only you don't eat sugar."

"Maybe they'll have fruit."

A sunny, warm, perfect day greeted them as they stepped outside the lodge.

Walking toward the van, Kate was struck by the irony of it all. The Black Hills had to be one of the most beautiful places in America, and yet John Howard was here to unleash unimaginable horrors on it. Why was he drawn to beauty? The base in Montana had been beautiful. Then there had been the op amidst the majesty of the Grand Canyon and the attack on the cruise ship in the Gulf of Mexico.

Confucius, Emerson, even Saint Augustine had all talked about the beauty of the world. But it was the quote by English environmentalist John Ray that Kate thought of as they walked from the lodge to the van. *Beauty is power; a smile is its sword.* John Howard had it backwards, though. He thought power was beauty, that a sword replaced a smile. He saw beauty and felt a need to defeat it.

They still didn't have phones or any type of GPS device, but Kate had taken one look at the map and memorized it. They passed The Rusty Spur Inn once without slowing down, continued on for another two blocks and pulled into the Calamity Jane Coffee Shop. Allison went in for their order, kept her baseball cap pulled low, and paid with cash.

She came back with three steaming coffees that smelled like life itself to Kate. She didn't even look in the bag of pastries until she'd taken two satisfying sips of the java. Allison was devouring a cinnamon roll larger than a personal-sized pizza.

When Kate looked in the bag and saw two more, she raised her eyebrows, she asked, "Sweet tooth?"

"There are nuts on top. It's protein!" Allison passed her a second bag which contained an overripe banana and a single-serving package of almonds.

The carbohydrates, protein, and caffeine cleared away any remaining cobwebs from Kate's brain.

Allison wiped the sugar from her fingertips and stuffed the napkin into her empty coffee cup. "I want to drive around the back of the inn."

"Chancy."

"What would they see? An old VW van. We hardly look like government agents in this thing."

"Okay." Kate's dread was morphing into anticipation. "We do one drive around the place. Only one, though I'm not really sure what we expect to see."

"Due diligence. We are obligated to check it out."

"And you're convinced this will not tip his hand."

"Not unless he steps in front of the van, then sees and identifies you from three feet."

"You are literally describing my worst nightmare."

"In which case, either run him over, or I'll jump out and shoot him."

"Or we could cuff him."

"I suppose."

"Let's do this."

"Absolutely."

Allison rolled up the bag with the two extra gargantuan cinnamon rolls and placed it in between the front seats, next to the extra cup of coffee. "Let's do this."

"Okay."

"Wait!" Allison unbuckled, jumped out of the van, and walked around to Kate's side.

"What's happening?"

"I'll drive."

"Because..."

"You have the perfect memory."

"It's not perfect. It's—"

"Eidetic. Whatever. You'll remember more than I will. If you see more, you'll remember more. I'll drive. You look. And remember."

"Right."

Five minutes later, they were pulling into the parking area of the Rusty Spur.

"Not a great place." Kate noticed peeling paint, some cars that looked as if they'd barely made it into the parking area, and a general air of neglect.

Allison maneuvered the van around a pothole. "John Howard is slumming it."

"Apparently."

They rounded the corner of the structure, which was single story and shaped like an L. Kate wondered if she should look at every license plate. Would it do any good to look them up later? Surely John had bought several sets of stolen plates—high market stuff where the vehicle would not have been reported missing. He had a wide variety of sources for such things. It was how the AT was able to operate.

As Allison drove toward the back of the building, Kate's gaze snagged on something red and shiny. Allison let out a gasp, but she didn't hit the brakes. She did nothing that would indicate she was surprised by what she'd seen.

Kate was trying to put together what she was staring at with what she knew about John Howard. Why would he have dared to be so bold? Was he losing his grip on reality and standard procedures and risk/loss analysis?

Allison pulled out onto the adjacent road, then drove in the opposite direction from their lodge.

"Where are you going?"

"Anywhere but straight home." Allison's gaze oscillated between the road and the rearview mirror. "I need to shake the feeling that he might have seen us."

"He didn't see us."

"I don't think so either."

"That was his vehicle."

"Probably."

"What was it?"

"A Voltaris X according to Donovan. We saw it yesterday."

"What?" Kate felt as if one more surprise wouldn't fit into her mind. "Where?"

"Headed toward Custer while Donovan and I were traveling toward the lodge."

"Wow."

"Yeah."

They were both silent for a moment as Allison drove out of town, then north and east, in order to wiggle her way back toward the lodge.

"It's like having a rattler crawl across the path in front of you," she said. "You realize after you see it how close it was to you. How deadly a thing it is."

"Has that happened to you?" Kate asked.

"Sure. Aunt Polly lives in Texas. Rattlers just come with the territory."

"That's awful."

"Exactly."

They come with the territory.

As did the likes of John Howard.

"Time to wake up Donovan," Allison said. "We have news to share."

"I'm not sure what it means. We already suspected he was in the area."

"True. But we could follow him now. Or we could enter his license plate into a program that you could write. Can you write a program like that?"

"I can. Wouldn't take more than a half hour at the most."

"Good. We'll track him virtually." Allison smiled broadly, almost a cat-caught-the-canary smile, which did a lot to settle Kate's nerves.

She never used to be like that—nervous, on edge, twitchy. That's what living with the AT had done to her. She supposed, as her therapist had suggested, she wasn't quite over it yet. She might never be over it.

But she was learning to live with the unsettled feelings.

Maybe, soon, she'd even learn how to use those same feelings to defeat the man behind the organization that had plagued America for too long. "We need to contact Reid Clark or Kendra Thomas or even Kenneth Langston."

"I'm still not sure about the wisdom of that." Allison's voice was tight, her eyes locked on the road in front of her.

"Because he might run?"

"Yes. We don't know where his backup sight is."

Kate surveyed the traffic—families in vans, men and women riding Harleys, even cyclists pedaling along the side of the road. All making their way toward one of the day's festivities. All at risk. "We have to, Allison. We can't sacrifice these people because it will bring us closer to our goal."

"Yeah." Allison slapped her hand against the steering wheel. "The problem is that John Howard has no qualms sacrificing people. He has no moral reservations. Maybe that's why he's always one step ahead of us."

"We can't become like him in order to defeat him."

"But what if that's the only way?" Now Allison looked at her, looked directly at Kate, and Kate remembered how personal this was for her friend.

"There will be another way."

They pulled up to a light and stopped next to a suburban.

Kate glanced over to see a young girl in large red, white, and blue sunglasses. The child waved, and Kate waved back. The parents had attached American flags to the tops of the backseat windows. They fluttered in the breeze, and Kate realized, suddenly, that it was Independence Day.

Of course, she'd known it was July 4th. She and Allison had both narrowed John's plans to this day, to the founding of a nation and the celebration of the stars and stripes.

America's birthday.

The light changed, and Allison pulled away from the car holding the little family. But in that moment, something in Kate changed. All of her hesitation fell away. All of her doubts and fears evaporated, and in their place, she experienced a rock-solid resolve.

They would contact their boss, and whether he believed them, whether he could send reinforcements or not, they would do everything in their power to stop the AT.

They would pay the price, whatever it was, to make this country a safe place—land of the free and home of the brave.

Let freedom ring.

Chapter Eleven

Donovan agreed with Kate. "It's time to call this in. Break radio silence. See what the boss says."

"But we agreed to do that if and when we had *irrefutable* evidence," Allison said. "Is this that?"

They both looked to Kate, who knew John Howard and the AT organization better than anyone on the task force.

"We have the suspicious tower hopping activity—performed with a skill that few organizations could achieve. We also have the Voltaris. What other cyber-terrorist could afford a vehicle like that?"

"But it might not be Howard," Allison argued. "Any of America's two percenters could have purchased that car."

Donovan sat back and smiled. "Yes, but only someone like John Howard would purchase that car, drive it to this town, and spend the night in a cheap motel."

Which settled it. They were convinced.

The question was whether their boss would be.

Allison drove to a pay phone at an old gas station on the outskirts of Custer. She called the number that they so rarely used —the one that had been programmed to bounce off half a dozen satellites before landing on a phone in a room at headquarters that was staffed 24 hours a day. Instead of transferring the call, the agent on duty said, "Please hold," then sent another agent out of the room to come back with the supervisor on site. She was relieved to hear Reid Clark's voice on the other end. He sounded gruff, on edge, tired. "What have you got?"

Allison summarized where they were, what they had found, and what they were certain would happen next.

Reid wasn't convinced. "You are three of my best agents, or I wouldn't have agreed to this mission or your strategy for it."

She heard the *however* coming before he said it.

"However, what you have isn't enough. It is not positive confirmation."

"It's not like we can snap a photo and send it to you since we have no cell phones."

"And I understand your reasons for that, but you don't even have eyes on, and before you repeat yourself, eyes on a vehicle that isn't supposed to be available yet isn't good enough." He sighed heavily, then asked, "Have you followed current news at all?"

"Negative."

"The attack on cellular devices has increased. There have been more casualties in the last twenty-four hours. Public transportation remains at a standstill. Congress and the President are demanding answers and resolutions. Right now, we can't give them either."

"How does that relate to this?"

The answer was both bristly and apologetic. "We're spread thin, that's how."

Silence filled the line.

Allison waited as her boss considered what she'd told him and placed it in context to what was happening in the rest of the nation. Finally, he said, "You get eyes on John Howard, and I'll redirect agents to your location. That's the best I can do."

"And until then?"

"Watch yourself." His voice grew suddenly softer. "No one questions your commitment and doggedness. We've been through a lot together—you, Donovan, Kate and myself. Just do me a personal favor and be careful."

And then he signed off.

Allison returned to the lodge and updated Kate and Donovan. It was ten-thirty in the morning by the time they'd gathered all their belongings and moved both vehicles to the service entry at the rear of the building. Parked with the backs of the vehicles nearly touching the sides of two trash dumpsters, they felt well hidden. The lodge appeared deserted. All of the guests had already split. They were out celebrating the holiday. All of the employees were preparing for the onslaught of hungry and exhausted tourists.

They'd left nothing in the rooms.

Kate had even disassembled and packed up her Faraday cage. In the end, it made no sense to write a computer program that would monitor the movement of the Voltaris. If they left Kate in the room to watch the program, they would have one less agent to capture him. And for what? She wouldn't be able to warn Allison or Donovan if the Voltaris was headed directly toward them.

Unless they broke their no tech pledge. Doing so seemed more of a risk than a benefit. Ditching technology had helped them make it as far as they were, but stopping a coordinated attack on two locations with only two agents wouldn't be possible. They needed Kate.

"We know what to look for," Donovan had reasoned. "That car will stick out like a sore thumb."

"More like a diamond in the rough." Allison nudged his shoulder. "Sorry. I know how much sports cars mean to you."

"I still can't believe he drove right by us." Donovan shook his head in frustration. "Damned tinted windows."

They were standing in between the two vehicles, doing a final supply check—firearms, extra mags, first aid kits, night optics, compass, map, zip ties, and restraint rope. Each vehicle also had a backpack containing water bottles, protein bars, and caffeine tablets. Caffeine tablets and rope? They weren't exactly planning a dash through the Black Hills. Allison didn't see herself following John Howard into the woods, but then again, she probably would if he was desperate enough to flee in that direction.

They'd packed everything else they owned into the back of each vehicle because the odds were high that they would not be returning to the lodge. What went unspoken between them was the certainty that by that evening, either they'd be dead or John Howard would. Somehow, Allison didn't see him as the type of terrorist who would throw up his arms and say, "You got me."

No.

John Howard would fight until the end.

She'd met his kind before.

Was he the man who had killed her father? Or was he the person who had hired the killer? Now that they were nearly at the final hour, she could see some things more clearly. Things that Donovan, Kate, and even Reid Clark had tried to talk to her about. Things she hadn't been willing to hear until now. Mainly, that John Howard might not have been the one who killed her father. John's military record established he was fifty-one years old. He worked in military intelligence in 1997. He would have been twenty-eight years old at the time of her father's murder, but he couldn't be two places at once, and his service record clearly established he'd been overseas at the time. She knew all too well that records could be changed.

A more critical question was, why would he have killed Arthur Quinn?

John's path had deviated when his family was murdered. He'd been thirty when he married Lillian Holmes. Nearly ten years after that, his wife and daughter died in an explosion planted by a foreign operative. John Howard didn't turn to the dark side until 2014 at the earliest, and more than likely, it had been several years later.

The timeline didn't match up.

And yet there was a connection between her father's murder and the Anarchists for Tomorrow. She was certain of that. If it wasn't John Howard, then it was someone else crucial to the organization. Who had been sending her the Tolkien texts? Stella Gonzalez? There was a possibility that the murderer could be the AT's financier. Allison honestly didn't know, though in her memory—in her dreams—it had always been a man. She'd been nine years old on the evening her father had been shot and killed. A child. And children's memories were imperfect. Adults' memories were only marginally better.

It could have been a woman. Allison didn't know, and she didn't care. All that mattered was apprehending his killer and making sure that he or she spent the rest of their days behind bars.

"You okay?" Kate asked.

"Peachy keen."

"Never heard her say that before." Donovan spoke in a mock whisper.

"I've never heard anyone say that before. Maybe I read it in a book back in high school."

"I'm fine." Allison appreciated their concern. She really did. But she was ready, more than ready, to get on with this mission. "I promise you. I am fine. Eager—that's all."

"Okay." Donovan tossed his backpack into the VW van. "One more time. Does anyone see a better way of doing this?"

Allison shook her head.

Kate said, "Actually I'm good with the plan. John's psychological profile says he always hits the biggest target. That will be Mount Rushmore."

"If we're correct and he stages a pre-emptive attack, Crazy Horse will be hit first. I don't like it. I don't like you being there alone." Allison waited for Kate to meet her gaze. "Promise that you'll be in contact with Larson."

"Definitely. The more people we have on our side, the better our chances. I'm convinced we can trust Larson and his crew. I'll contact them first thing before I approach the Crazy Horse site."

"You and Larson at Crazy Horse. Allison and I at Mount Rushmore. Use your state identification—"

"The ones with our aliases."

"Right. We'll use those to contact the persons in charge at each site. Don't alarm them, but put them on a high alert status. We don't want the sites closed, but we need to be notified if they see anything of concern."

"Notified how?" Kate asked. "We don't have cell phones."

"Let them copy your ID with the fake names but the correct picture, and distribute it among the staff. If anyone sees anything, they should alert you. Also, we won't have any way to contact each other, but we will be surrounded by people with cell phones. If anyone hears that something has occurred at the other site, hold your position as long as you're needed there. The first attack will be a diversionary one."

"Copy that," Kate said.

Allison nodded, started to speak, stopped herself, then started again. "We cannot view our mission as having a primary and secondary objective. Both objectives are equally important. We catch John Howard and the remaining members of the AT, and we prevent future casualties. We stop today's attack, and we only prevent today's casualties. If we sacrifice the first goal for the second, we will only succeed in kicking the can down the road. Remember, this may be the best scenario we ever have. This may be as close as we ever get to chopping the head off the snake."

And though they were professionals, armed and ready for combat, Donovan pulled both her and Kate into a tight circle. Their heads touched in what felt ridiculously like a huddle. Allison breathed in the smell of them, the scent of friendship and trustworthiness and loyalty. She allowed herself one brief moment of appreciating everything she had in that moment, and then she pulled away, climbed into the VW, and set her mind on the mission ahead.

When they pulled into the Mount Rushmore parking garage, the place was even more crowded than the day before. Donovan only found a place to park because a family with three small children pointed to their spot. When Donovan rolled down his window, an exhausted mom admitted, "We're headed to our hotel for a nap. You can have our spot."

Allison had carefully surveyed the parked cars as they drove to the top floor of the parking garage, and from the top of the structure, they spent a good ten minutes looking out over the entire area. No red Voltaris.

"Why would he drive such a conspicuous car?" Donovan asked.

"Hubris. Defined as excessive pride, presumption or arrogance."

"In Howard's case, probably all three."

They walked down the stairs of the parking garage and pushed their way through the crowd.

Allison didn't know what she'd expected to see, but whatever it was—she didn't. Nothing nefarious. No hints as to the carnage that might be lurking around the next corner. Instead, she saw a large-sized crowd enjoying a summer celebration. Kids with popsicles, sodas, popcorn, even cotton candy. A vendor cooking hotdogs. Parents looking exhausted, though it wasn't yet noon.

They made their way to the viewing platform. The memorial was still there—all four presidents looking out across the Black Hills as they had since 1941. The monolith remained. Tourists took pictures, videos, and selfies of both the monument and the monolith.

No terrorists skulking in the shadows that she could see.

No immediate threat.

"Let's check in with Moss," Donovan suggested.

"I am sure he'll be happy to see us again."

He wasn't. The director looked even more harried than the day before. His uniform was ruffled, his hair—what there was of it—unkempt. He barely glanced up from a sheaf of papers he was moving from one side of his desk to the other. "I'm afraid I don't have much time."

"Doing paperwork?" Allison didn't even try to keep the sarcasm out of her voice.

Moss caught on to that, put his hand flat against the stack of papers, smiled to himself, then looked up at her. "*For every minute spent organizing, an hour is earned.* Benjamin Franklin said that. I've found it to be true."

Allison resisted the urge to roll her eyes or throttle him.

"We met yesterday," Donovan reminded the park director.

"Yes. I remember. And now you're back."

"We are."

"I still can't imagine why the state police would send two people here on the busiest weekend of the year."

He waited for them to fill in the reason *why*, which they did not do.

Instead, Allison sat in the chair across from Moss and waited for Donovan to do the same. Moss quit fiddling with his stack of papers. They'd caught his attention finally. That was something.

"How many staff do you have working today?" Allison asked.

He sat back, exasperated. "Twenty-four. A full twenty percent more than normal."

"All security?" Donovan asked.

"Well, no. Of course not. Some are cashiers, waitresses, cooks. We certainly don't have twenty-four security guards or park rangers. We have eight, and five of them are working today."

"Call in the other three." Allison leaned forward.

"Why?"

"We can't tell you why."

"I'm just supposed to believe you?"

"Yes."

"I don't suppose the state will pick up the cost."

"Forget the cost."

"Easy for you to say, though you're not actually saying much at all. You're giving me no real reason for such a move."

Allison threw an exasperated look at Donovan, who shrugged.

"Our word isn't good enough?" she asked.

"Our being here should be reason enough," Donovan offered.

"But why are you here? Because of the monoliths? How are

they a danger to anyone? A nuisance—yes. An affront to the historical integrity of this park and a blemish to the area's natural beauty. But they're not inherently dangerous, and we certainly don't need extra security because of a monolith."

Allison blew out a large breath. "I can't give you any specifics. I can tell you we have reason to believe there may be an attack here today."

This caused Moss to sit up straighter. "An attack. What kind of attack?"

"The kind where people die."

"Then why hasn't the state police been called? Or more of your people? Why have I not heard of this from the National Park Service Director or the secretary of the Department of Homeland Security?"

Allison felt her patience about to snap. People like Moss made her job exponentially harder.

"Would you consider closing?" Donovan asked.

They certainly didn't want that to happen because John Howard would switch to his back-up site. But they had to catch this man's attention, and Allison understood that was the reason for Donovan's question.

"I would not. Unless you have something more concrete to show me. I can't close every time some—" He stopped himself, seemed at a loss to choose the correct word that he was clearly intent on applying to them. "I can't close every time there's an unsubstantiated threat."

"Have you had previous unsubstantiated threats?" Donovan asked.

Moss waved that question away. "It's our busiest day of the year. Unless you can give me concrete evidence of a threat and unless I can substantiate that evidence with my boss, then no—I most certainly would not consider closing."

"Fine," Donovan said, clearly not surprised. "Then at least call in your extra personnel."

Moss didn't look convinced.

"We don't have time to argue with you," Allison said. "If something happens today, and you didn't take every precaution, you will be held responsible—maybe not in a court of law, but certainly in the court of public opinion."

He studied them a moment, then pulled out a perfectly folded white handkerchief and patted at the sweat on his brow. "Okay. Fine. You win. I'll have my assistant do it right now."

"Not your assistant. Don't give any specifics to anyone."

"I don't know any specifics."

"You make the calls," Donovan continued. "You don't have to explain. Just tell them crowds are larger than expected—"

"Which they are," Allison reminded him.

"Ask them to come in and stay until close."

"That's ten hours." Moss visibly bristled now, indignant. "We can't afford that kind of overtime."

Which was when Allison realized he wasn't merely a paper-pusher. He was a penny pincher, too. She supposed it was to be expected in government jobs, but she had no patience for bureaucratic concerns at the moment.

She stood, straightened her shirt so that he would see her holster, met his gaze when he looked up at her. Surprised? Half the people in South Dakota were carrying, and he was surprised? What world did this guy live in?

"Call them. Get them in here. Tell all of your security people that you need them to work until close. Draw up a schedule where each person gets a thirty-minute-break every three hours. They need to stay sharp, and they can't do that unless they're given regular breaks."

Donovan remained seated. He leaned forward, tapped Moss's desk, and waited for the man to look at him. "You have our images in your security system. Send our pictures and our names out to your entire detail. If they see anything that is suspect, anything at all, one of your people should find us."

"Find you?"

"We'll be on property."

"Why can't they just call you?"

Donovan stood, loomed over the desk, got right up in Moss's face. "In case you haven't heard, cell phones are blowing up all over America. We're not carrying one. Got it?"

Moss actually pushed his chair back away from his desk, apparently eager to put a little distance between himself and Donovan Steele. "Yes. Of course."

They turned and walked out of the room.

"Could have gone worse," Allison said.

"Yup. And it could have gone better."

Tanner Red Cloud Larson definitely understood the seriousness of the situation. His first recommendation was that Kate meet with onsite members of the Cow Creek Sioux Tribe, who shared security details with Larson's group at the Crazy Horse Memorial. Morley Swanson was a little older than Larson, quite a bit rounder, and had the same serious, taking-it-all-in demeanor.

Kate laid out the current situation as simply as possible, at least the parts she could share. In other words, short on details but big on the overall dangers.

Swanson raised a hand to stop her from continuing. "The CEO of the foundation is on-site today. Let's bring him in, as well as Mr. Ziolkowski."

Kate looked to Larson, who nodded once.

Ten minutes later she found herself in a larger conference room, surrounded by more people than she had envisioned briefing. In for a dime, in for a dollar as her father used to say.

Larson and three of his people joined the meeting. All other Lakota Sioux security personnel were currently on patrol or monitoring drone footage. Morley Swanson rejoined them, bringing with him two additional members from the Cow Creek Sioux Tribe.

Also joining them was Stoney Speidel, the CEO of Crazy

Horse Memorial Foundation, and Noah Ziolkowski, who was also on the foundation's board. Ziolkowski was an active engineer on the site, and a relative of Korczak Ziolkowski, the original sculptor of the Crazy Horse Memorial.

Nine plus Kate. She thought they made a promising team.

It wasn't everyone who would be affected by the day's events. She was painfully aware of that fact. Thousands of tourists milled around beyond the room—eating at the restaurant, strolling through the museum, shopping for that special gift to take home. The employees were doing their best to make every person's visit a good one, but the employees had not planned for John Howard.

Larson updated them on the status of the monolith closest to Crazy Horse and shared that he had four men in custody.

"Do you plan to hand them over to the feds?" Swanson asked.

Larson deferred to Kate.

"That will be determined at another time."

Swanson blinked, which was probably the equivalent of a gasp for most people. "As in today or tomorrow, I hope, since we can only legally detain someone without charging them for twenty-four to forty-eight hours. In addition, there's a very narrow scope regarding situations where we can charge a non-tribal member."

"We usually do transfer custody to federal agencies," Speidel added.

Ziolkowski said nothing. Simply watched and listened.

"I understand the constraints of tribal law," Kate said. "The Indian Civil Rights Act of 1968 as well as the Tribal Law and Order Act of 2010 both explicitly spell out those limitations."

Swanson and Speidel exchanged a glance, probably surprised that she was aware of the exact intersections of tribal law with the U.S. Constitution. Kate could have quoted those laws to them, line by line, since she'd looked at it in the weeks leading up to their trip to South Dakota—looked at it, and, of course, remembered everything.

Instead of explaining about her eidetic memory, she moved

the discussion straight into the current crisis. "The men in Mr. Lawson's custody were attempting to remove both the monolith at Mount Rushmore and the one outside of this facility."

"Notice they didn't put it on the grounds of this facility. Our security is tighter than Mount Rushmore's. That may sound boastful, but it's a simple face." Speidel looked to Ziolkowski.

The man drummed his fingertips against the table, then cleared his throat. "The Crazy Horse Memorial sits on private land managed by a nonprofit organization. While our rights are limited to this property, we have fewer restrictions. We maintain exclusive authority here, which includes the legal right to decide who can access the property as well as when they may do so. We also have more latitude in regard to surveillance, which we have taken full advantage of. We can immediately remove anyone we deem a threat, and we can enforce specific rules. All of this we can do outside of public scrutiny, unlike our friends at Mount Rushmore."

He met her gaze, didn't rush her, didn't look away.

Kate understood what he was saying, but she also understood that he didn't have the complete picture. And she couldn't give it to him.

"In spite of the fact that this land is private, we believe it may be targeted today."

"Who is *we*?" This from a woman working under Morley Swanson, ostensibly a member of the Cow Creek Sioux Tribe.

Kate realized it was now or never.

She needed to be very careful, but this might be the only chance she had to issue a very clear warning—one that could, ostensibly, save lives.

"I can't answer that question. I can show you my ID, as I've shown Mr. Larson, but I will tell you up front that it's a false identity. My partners and I are working under aliases so that we can keep our information out of the data net. Otherwise, they—the people planning this attack—will know we're here."

"Data is a curious word to use," Speidel said. "Data sounds

like numbers and facts, but what is being collected by our government as well as big tech is much more than that. The network of satellites that encircle the globe steal all of our information without our permission and use it as the owners of the network see fit."

"Exactly. More pertinent to this discussion, those networks can and have been hacked."

No one seemed surprised.

Kate had the feeling it would take a lot to surprise these people. "My partners are at Mount Rushmore, where we expect the main attack will take place. I'm here. Warning you."

"Why hasn't the government sent reinforcements?" Swanson asked. "Why haven't they suggested we close the facility today?"

"The government, per my boss, is spread thin with the increased attacks on cellular devices and the immobilization of public transportation. Also, they don't believe that the evidence we have is conclusive."

"Ah," said Swanson. "Clearly, you believe it is."

"I do."

"You believe this facility is at risk?"

"Yes."

"So you're here, alone, to warn us."

"Yes."

Now Ziolkowski and Speidel glanced at one another—a smile tugging at the corners of their lips. Then, Speidel said something in a low voice which everyone except Kate understood.

"What am I missing?" she asked Larson.

"Speidel shared that in the past, the federal government sent troops of men. This time they have sent one woman. Perhaps they are growing wiser."

"My heart tells me that you speak honestly," Speidel said. "Please continue."

She told them that the attack on Crazy Horse would be a diversionary one—something to require the services of local police and EMS. Once the first responders were on site, the attack on Mount Rushmore would take place.

"How certain are you of this?" Ziolkowski asked.

"If I were forced to put a number on it—ninety-seven percent."

"That's quite exact."

"It is."

He nodded once. "It says much of your commitment and integrity that you are here. Obviously, you consider such an attack —here, today—to be a likely scenario."

"I do."

Swanson frowned. "What you're saying is that our workers, as well as those visiting this site, may be at risk."

"Yes."

"Why not bring in the National Guard?"

"No one wants that sort of optics on this."

"That's what we're worried about?"

"It's what my boss's boss would be worried about."

"We could simply close the site," Ziolkowski said.

"Yes. You could, and I don't have the authority to stop you. Perhaps you should. But if you do, the perpetrators will simply move their attack to a back-up site. We don't know where that is. We would have no way to warn those people, as we're now warning you."

Silence filled the room. It was Larson who quietly, gently reminded them, "Crazy Horse wished to die fighting. Today we may be given that opportunity."

Kate excused herself to use the ladies' room. Mainly, she wanted to give them a few minutes of privacy to reach a consensus. It didn't take long. When she returned, they were ready to continue the briefing.

Speidel said, "We will bring in as many extra people as we can. People to watch, protect, and if need be—respond."

"Thank you."

"What will you do?" Swanson asked.

"Me? I'm going to catch the bastard."

Which seemed to satisfy everyone. No one asked how one woman could catch a terrorist or group of terrorists bent on destruction. No one questioned why she didn't have a cell phone whereby they could contact her.

"I'll be on site," she assured them. "Send my picture out to your workers. If you need me for any reason, have someone bring me in."

Ziolkowski had one additional request before the meeting broke up. "Do you have a timeline?"

"The Mount Rushmore attack will probably coincide with the fireworks show. This attack would precede that by one to two hours."

"What is your rough estimate?"

"Twilight ends at fifteen minutes past nine. The purpose of the attack here will be to divert all first responders. I'd guess one to two hours before."

Ziolkowski considered that for a moment. "I would like for you to update us at five p.m."

"I can do that."

"Should you still believe that this attack will happen, at that time we will make a decision whether to empty the campus." He held up his hand before she could argue. "We'll be working on a plan to do so inconspicuously."

Kate cocked her head, studied him, then nodded. "Understood."

Ziolkowski thanked her for informing them and promised to find her and report back if they saw anything suspicious.

It was Speidel who stepped in front of her as those assembled hurried off to their assigned positions. "*It does not take many words to tell the truth.* This is a saying handed down in my tribe, and it applies here today. Thank you for telling us the truth."

"Thank you for listening."

And then he said something that both touched her heart and bolstered her courage.

"May the Great Spirit walk with you."

It had been a long time since Kate had thought about God, about her faith, about the things that she believed. Somehow, during her time working for John Howard, she'd had to lock any such considerations into a hidden part of her heart and mind. Now, she wasn't sure what she believed. But when she stepped back outside, stepped back into the sunshine and the crowds and the celebrations, she couldn't help uttering a silent prayer that the God of her youth, the God of her parents, and the Lakota's Great Spirit would protect these people.

Larson accompanied her as she made her way back to the Bronco. "Where will you go now?"

"I'd like to go up to the actual memorial and have a look around."

"Ziolkowski thought you might say that. There's an employee in the four-wheeler ... the one there in front of the bus. He'll take you up."

She turned and shook Larson's hand. "Thank you. I have a feeling that went well because you stood beside me."

Larson smiled, looked down at the ground, and then back up at her. "It went well because you speak with knowledge and compassion. This has not always been the case between your people and ours."

"Yeah. I suppose not."

"I'd like a quicker way to get in touch with you," he said. "Walkie talkies?"

Kate shook her head. "They'll be scanning frequencies. Smoke signals?"

He laughed. "Maybe we could put a big red hat on you so that you'd stand out in the crowd."

"Most people who work for my agency don't want to stand out in a crowd. They definitely don't wear red hats." She stepped closer and lowered her voice, as if someone nearby might be listening.

Who was to say? Howard could have directional mics placed

around the facility. If so, then he was probably halfway to Canada by now. Still, she felt better lowering her voice.

"I'll go up to the memorial, check out the workers and the area. Can you send a couple of your people to monitor every road and path between the memorial and the visitor's center?"

"Yes."

"Look for any signs of buried explosives, check places that might hide a cache of weapons, report back with anything at all that looks out of place."

"We'll do it."

"Thank you."

"Of course."

Larson walked away, and Kate reached into the backseat of the Bronco for her backpack, wound her arms through it, locked the vehicle, and walked toward the four-wheeler. As she climbed into the vehicle, she could practically hear John Howard's countdown clock ticking its way toward darkness and death and destruction.

Chapter Twelve

John squeezed the bridge of his nose, trying to beat back the beginnings of a tension headache.

Jasmine continued cowering over her laptop, trying to figure out what had become of the monolith removal work crews.

"Start at the beginning," he said in a gentler voice than he customarily used. He could rise to the occasion. It was possible that choking her earlier had been a mistake. She'd lost her spunkiness, and if there was one thing cyber-terrorists needed, it was spunkiness. He couldn't afford to let her spiral down the drain now. If Jasmine needed a little hand holding, he could do that. After all, Jasmine and Spencer were the only two employees he had left. The others had met a convenient end.

"We've been tracking the new vehicle we purchased them, as well as their cell phones." With a shaking finger, she pointed to a dot on the map displayed on her monitor. "Here you can see where they parked the van along an adjacent back road near Mount Rushmore. They walked toward the monolith, stayed there about forty minutes—"

She hesitated, so John said, "Forty minutes sounds about right."

"I thought so too." Her voice gained a small degree of confidence as she spoke.

John felt reassured that Jasmine would be just fine. After all, he only needed her a little longer. He peeked at his watch which read 1407. Sunset would be at 2041 hour. Twilight ended at 2115 and the action was set to begin a few minutes after that. Jasmine needed to hold it together for another eight, maybe nine, hours.

He waited for her to continue. When she didn't, he prompted with "You thought forty minutes made sense, but..."

"When they get back to the vehicle, they sit there for a few minutes. Does that seem strange?"

"It does, since they didn't have a monolith to load up."

"Maybe they were trying to figure out what to do next. But if they were on site, *why* didn't they pick up the monolith?"

"Too much additional security would be my bet." Spencer didn't even look up. He kept pecking away at his keyboard like a happy little hen. "Scoped it out, decided they'd be apprehended, so they go back to the van and discuss what to do next."

"Or they were arrested," Stella said, rattling her ice cubes and taking another gulp of her drink.

John had hoped she would take a nap, but Stella seemed remarkably perky for someone her age who had drank a lot of scotch the night before.

"I thought of that, too." Jasmine clicked the mouse and the time lapse track of the henchmen's movement continued. "But they get into the van and drive to the monolith near Crazy Horse. Once again, they access a back road. They're there for over an hour, and then they leave."

"Without the monolith," Stella chirped. "We know that from all the news coverages of the monoliths this morning."

"These scenes are both super hot!" Spencer sounded almost gleeful—as if to say *mission accomplished*. "Be grateful they were smart enough to leave the monoliths in place. If they had been caught, they'd crack faster than an egg dropped on a sizzling skillet."

"Where do our contractors go after that?" John asked, attempting to keep the impatience out of his voice and failing.

Jasmine's hand began to shake again on top of the mouse, and it took her a few tries to actually click the device. "Umm ... they go northeast to Rapid City and stop outside of the Pennywise Motel. Their vehicles and cell phones haven't moved since."

"Have you tried calling them?" Stella again shook the ice in her glass and moved closer to the table so that she could peer over Jasmine's shoulder.

"I did. The phones are turned off."

"As they should be." John stepped away from the table, more to get away from the stench of Stella's scotch than anything else. The Macallan had been delicious, but he did not think this was the appropriate time for drinking. If Stella needed a little pickup to help her through the day, he'd provided pills for that.

Jasmine looked as if the word BOO would send her into convulsions.

Spencer seemed a little too cocky.

And Stella had made a *harrumph* sound, then returned to her room to replenish her drink.

He needed some time out of these motel rooms.

Snatching up the fob to the Voltaris, he walked with the attention and speed of a man who had an important appointment. His father had once told him to "walk as if you have someplace to be." Funny that he should remember his old man now. They'd never been close.

He felt better the minute he sank into the leather seats of the Voltaris. There was nothing like a luxury vehicle to soothe a man's nerves. He drove out of Custer, north on 385, past the monolith that was supposed to be gone. Well, anything could explain that. People were not always trustworthy. Perhaps the people he'd hired didn't care for the intense scrutiny of both the public and law enforcement. Maybe they'd experienced cold feet. Jasmine had found nothing on the police scanners to indicate they'd been arrested, and it would undoubtedly make the news if that had happened.

He sped north, letting the speedometer ease ten, then twenty over the posted speed. A feeling of exhilaration replaced his earlier gloom as he passed the exit for Crazy Horse Memorial. Spencer could be trusted to carry out that part of today's festivities. Both Spencer's psychological profile and his reactions since coming to work for the AT indicated that he could be easily manipulated.

Spencer wanted to feel important.

He needed to see himself near the top of the pyramid.

He couldn't envision things not going his way, which is why it would be necessary to kill him after the Crazy Horse Memorial bombing.

John's confidence grew as he continued north, though he prudently reduced the speed of the Voltaris. A speeding ticket could ruin his plans. The attacks might continue, but the crowning achievement, the decisive blow, was something that only he could deliver.

"We came here once. Do you remember?"

He glanced at the passenger seat.

Lillian.

It had been weeks, possibly months, since he'd seen her. Immediately following her murder, she'd appeared to him almost every day, but that had been such a very long time ago. He'd missed her. Feared he wouldn't see her again. And now, he worried that if he spoke, if he did anything to break the magic of the moment, she would disappear.

"You remember, John. Right?" She tucked her blonde hair behind her ear, smiled at him, then looked back out the window.

"I always wished that we could move here. Maybe after you retired. Have a home on a small rise that looked out over the Black Hills. Nothing showy, but not small either." She laughed, and the joy in John's heart felt as if it would overflow, like a river breaking free of its banks.

He cleared his voice, swallowed back the tears, and said, "Procida is even more lovely than South Dakota—colorful buildings, a laid-back vibe, but still there's culture there. And the cuisine." He kissed his fingertips and said, "Mwa!" Lillian had always laughed when he'd done that. He looked over to see her reaction, then shook his head.

She was gone.

Had it been a dream? Was he hallucinating again? The online shrink had assured him that the pills would stop the visions as long as he avoided stress.

Then he heard Penelope's sweet voice.

"Are we there yet, Daddy?"

He glanced in the rearview mirror. Saw her safely buckled in her car seat. "Almost, baby."

"I'm not a baby."

"Oh, yes. I forgot." Only four years old and yet so precocious.

"I like the beach," she said.

"You do?"

"Yup. I like the shells. And the waves that go crash. And playing in the sand."

"You can do all of those things in Procida."

He'd been watching the road, the speedometer, even slowing a little to see the line of cars still pouring off the main road, hurrying toward Mount Rushmore. It was as if the herd of sheep referred to as the American public couldn't get there fast enough. They were hoping to see a spectacular fireworks show. He was going to provide that and more!

How would they react to the RPGs?

How would they respond to his message?

Some would be sacrificed to the bioagent. It was a shame, but necessary. His gaze returned to the rearview mirror again, hoping to see Penelope, but he was alone.

Not surprising.

Good things didn't last, and life at the top was lonely.

For now, he needed to focus on the mission. He needed to

make sure that everything went off without a hitch. He needed to do it for Lillian and for Penelope.

Allison's frustration grew as the sun moved to the west. What was left of daylight filtered through a forest of trees. She glanced at her watch. Fifteen minutes after four. Five hours until the fireworks show.

If anything, the number of tourists had increased. The park store was filled with people queued up, waiting to purchase mugs and hats and t-shirts and keychains. Families crammed into the restaurant booths and spilled out onto the terrace. The Presidential Trail was filled with children running ahead of parents, couples holding hands as they strolled down the path, and harried park workers.

In other words, the place looked like any iconic American tourist attraction on a national holiday.

"I checked in with Moss," Donovan said, walking up to her and pushing a hotdog into her hands. "Eat this."

"You brought me lunch?"

He shrugged, so she bit into the hotdog—mustard and ketchup, relish, a piping hot weenie, and a fresh bun. Donovan had even remembered to add crumbled up chips and a touch of cheese across the top. She might have groaned.

"Right?" He grinned, then handed her a drink.

Coca-Cola—the real stuff, not a diet derivative. She finished the hot dog in four bites, gulped down the entire soda. The carbs hit her system like a freight train. When had she last eaten? "Thanks."

"Sure."

"No, I mean really thanks. Didn't realize how hungry I was."

"Getting a little hangry?"

"I don't get hangry."

He drummed his fingertips against his lips and wiggled his

eyebrows. She hadn't much missed her cell phone, but she wished she had it now. She wanted to commit this moment to memory. Donovan standing there, smiling at her, Mount Rushmore in the distance, and a thousand American patriots in between. Would she look back and remember this as the moment before everything went terribly, terribly wrong?

"Hey." His voice was still joking, but his expression had turned suddenly serious—concerned even.

When was the last time someone had been concerned about her? Aunt Polly. Edward. Kate. Reid. Donovan. She had a small but loyal circle.

"Are you okay? Because I can go get another hot dog."

"How can you joke?"

"It's how some mortals handle pressure." He nodded over to a recently vacated bench.

Allison knew that sitting for even a moment would be a mistake. The last rays of the sun, a full stomach, and a suddenly active digestive system all added up to a cat nap, which she had no intention of taking. "Let's walk," she suggested.

They made their way down the Presidential Trail, that was basically a half-mile loop. They had both already walked it half a dozen times—maybe more, and they'd come up with absolutely zero. What had John Howard meant when he'd told Clint to stay off the trail? Because of the surveillance? Or because he'd planted something there? Were they, even now, walking by a planted bomb? Where were the closest bomb-sniffing dogs, and how fast could they be transported to the Mount Rushmore location?

It was insane to put these people at risk.

They needed to pull the plug on the day's festivities.

Not that it was her decision.

Clarence Moss would not be an easy man to convince.

Portions of the trail were wheelchair accessible, but other parts included stairs and boardwalks. Donovan and Allison walked around families that were occupied with the simplest tasks of life—a mother pulling a child from a stroller, an older woman pushing grandpa in his wheelchair, parents wearily reminding children to slow down, teens pretending to be disinterested, though even they stopped to take selfies.

There were less of the *QuantumGuard Pouches* here. She didn't know if that was because they felt safer on national park property or if they simply were tired of being vigilant.

Donovan noticed her gaze and pulled her to the side of the trail, where they had a modicum of privacy. "Are you worried about the cell phones?"

"I'm worried about everything, including the fact that we haven't seen one thing out of the ordinary."

"Doesn't mean we're wrong."

"No. It doesn't."

They caught their first break ten minutes later in the form of a twenty-something kid with a scrawny beard, wearing a University of South Dakota t-shirt, and carrying an old-fashioned camera. It wasn't old-fashioned, not in the sense of using 35mm film. The kid's camera was a digital device, but he could still fiddle with the aperture and shutter speed. The fact that he stood in the middle of the path, staring down at the image on the screen, frowning, and biting his lip, caught Donovan's attention.

"Problem?" Donovan asked.

"Maybe." He looked up, glanced at Allison, then Donovan, then back down at his camera.

"I'm Allison. This is Donovan." She consciously made the decision to use their real names. There was no chance that this kid worked for John Howard. If he did, her instincts were so far off that she would do her country a favor by resigning.

"Oh. Hey. Gunner. Gunner France." He must have caught the look between them, because he smiled awkwardly. "I know. Trust me. I've received that reaction all of my life. Some days, I'd give my right arm to have a name like Joe Smith."

"So, Gunner France. What's the problem? Donovan and I are both pretty good with cameras."

"I can't tell what I'm looking at exactly, but it's something." He held the camera at arms-length so they could see.

The three stood there, staring at a picture of leaves.

"What were you taking a picture of, Gunner?"

"Western Tanager." Using the left arrow, he toggled back three photos.

The bird on the screen was medium-sized, with a yellow body, orange-red head, and black wings that held splashes of yellow.

"Definitely a male. First one I've photographed." His voice held a little awe. "I know it sounds geeky, but nature photography is actually a pretty cool major. And our first assignment was birds, so..."

"Western tanager." To Allison, it looked slightly larger than the finches on Aunt Polly's feeders back in Texas.

"Walk us through it," Donovan said.

Allison could hear the game clock ticking down in her head. They should be doing something more important than looking at Gunner France's camera. Then again, they'd made absolutely zero progress since arriving.

"I was walking down the trail, looking for anything that might be on our class list but not really expecting to find anything given the amount of people here."

"You're taking summer classes?"

"Yeah. Came here with my parents because they insisted on a family vacation. You know how it is." He shook his head as if to say that the logic of parents was beyond him. "I was pretty excited to see the tanager. Took an almost perfect shot of it, then it flitted to the right. I turned the camera and caught.... Well, you saw the terrible shot, but then something else caught my eye. That's the third shot, the first one I showed you."

"Looks like leaves," Allison said.

"Right?" The kid wasn't offended at all at the tone of Allison's voice. He forwarded back to the picture they had initially looked at.

Donovan saw it first. "Can you switch this photo to black and white?"

"Sure."

"Now zoom in on the top, right quadrant."

What was she looking at? What was that? And why was it in the tree?

Donovan locked eyes with Allison, then turned to Gunner. "Does your camera have wireless capability?"

"Nah. Professor Livingston insisted we order a model without it, given ... you know."

"Yeah. We know. Sim card?"

"Not a removable one. I have to—" He mimicked plugging a cord into the device.

Donovan dug a business card out of his wallet. There was nothing on it except an email address that appeared to be random numbers and letters. "Email it to me when you get back to school?"

"Okay."

"It's important."

"Oh."

"And Gunner..."

"Yeah?"

"Find your parents and get them out of here. Fake a stomach ache if you have to."

Donovan had Gunner's complete attention for the first time.

"Why would I do that?"

"Just do it, Gunner. And send me that picture—as soon as you're back home."

Allison's stomach tumbled. They could save Gunner and his parents, but how were they going to save all of the people teeming around them? And what had Donovan seen?

They continued walking until they'd moved a few yards off the trail where they wouldn't be overheard.

"Explain to me what we were looking at on Gunner's camera," Allison said.

"You're familiar with the military use of drones to deliver payloads?"

"Sure. They determine a target..."

"They paint a target, either with GPS coordinates or a laser beam provided by ground troops."

"Still not understanding."

"I think what Tanner photographed was the opposite of that."

"You think the AT has militarized drones?"

"Probably, but they wouldn't use them here. You and Kate were right. John Howard wants to experience this one up close and personal."

Maybe she hadn't slept enough. Maybe the heat was getting to her. Or maybe the amount of stress she'd been under for so very long—for what felt like her entire life—was muddling her brain.

"Stay with me," Donovan said. "He doesn't need to paint the target. He knows where the target is..."

Donovan put a hand on each of Allison's shoulders and turned her back toward the visitor's center. It was actually visible through the trees—though not well. Allison thought a shot with a rifle would be almost impossible. But someone with a handheld device, say an RPG or a Stinger—really any type of portable rocket launcher, could hit the complex even from the trees. If they stepped out into the open, almost anyone could do it, certainly someone with a minimal amount of training.

Donovan leaned closer and lowered his voice. "His shooter will have a handheld receiver that will ping what Gunner photographed in the tree. That tinsel is in exactly the right place from which to fire a missile that would land in the middle of the visitor center. All the shooter has to do is stand in the right location. Howard will have already programmed in the coordinates of the visitor center. It's not as sophisticated as a smart missile, but it's still pretty advanced. "

"All the shooter needs is to know the exact location where he needs to stand."

"Exactly. And it might not be under the tree. Their directions might be to find the location, ping the ribbon, then step forward five feet. It's simple math."

"It looked like tinsel."

"I've seen it on the research boards. Goes by different names —FlashLine is the closest to production, but there's also Silver-Strike and TrailShimmer. It can paint a target or it can provide a location for the shooter to stand. Takes zero skill. Basically a point and shoot operation."

"Shoot what? RPGs?"

"Any small caliber missile. There's probably a long list. The beauty is that no one would notice a FlashLine, even if they looked up. It looked invisible until Gunner turned the photo to black and white, then the contrast picked up what our eyes couldn't."

"How did he—"

"Fate? Luck? I don't know, but Allison, this means that we're right. This is confirmation that the attack will be here today."

"We need to tell Clarence Moss."

"We need to call Reid."

Chapter Thirteen

John ordered the vehicle for Spencer—a BMW sports car. The kid deserved a little fun. He'd been working nonstop since.... Spencer had been freakishly focused for as long as he'd worked for the AT. Real shame he wouldn't live to enjoy the spoils of his labors. Still, he could have a hell of a last ride.

They were standing outside—standing between the Voltaris and the BMW. Stella was in the front seat of the Voltaris, complaining because she'd run out of liquor. Jasmine was in the back seat, still tapping away on her laptop.

"Let's go over it one more time," John said. "Specific locations were tagged?"

"Check."

"Shooters have received half of their payment."

"Check."

"You've preloaded the detonation program on their cellular devices and set a timer."

"It'll go off at midnight."

"Excellent. They'll either be home relaxing or out celebrating at a bar. Either way, no one will ever trace what's left of them back to us."

"Not a chance."

"Quinn and Steele?"

"Best guess—Mount Rushmore."

"Kate?"

"Nothing."

John sighed. Well, this wasn't Christmas. He couldn't reasonably expect to receive everything on his list.

"You understand your assignment?"

Spencer held up his phone, then grinned at the BMW. "Drive this baby to Crazy Horse. Use my phone to photograph the initial explosions."

"It'll be useful for social media later. We'll blame it on the government."

"Right." Spencer nodded so hard, the sunglasses perched on his head slipped to one side. "Once I've visually confirmed that the explosions detonated via their preset timers, I'll skedaddle."

"Wait there until you can confirm that the majority of the regional EMS vehicles show up."

"Of course."

"But don't let yourself be seen."

"I'm just another rich guy, gawking at the scene."

"Then meet us at Mount Rushmore. We'll be on the Presidential Trail, at the overlook. You're better at recording than Jasmine, so be sure and get there well before we go live."

"Got it."

John had the niggling suspicion that there was something he was forgetting. It wasn't the viral payload. That had been put in position at the tourist center weeks ago. No. It was something else he needed to prepare Spencer for. They were so close now. He couldn't allow the kid's naiveté ruin the mission. He raised his gaze, stared out over the small town of Custer and tried to envision what could go wrong. They'd planned every detail. Prepared for every contingency. One reason he was so successful was that he meticulously worked through every possible scenario. That, and he didn't underestimate his adversaries.

His adversaries.

Katelyn Ballou.

The only player in this game of chess that he could not account for. The woman with an eidetic memory, a remarkable IQ, and enough courage to work against him right under his nose. If he didn't want so badly to kill her, he'd invite her to join him for a glass of celebratory champagne afterwards. Together, they would have made a good team—an unstoppable team.

Instead, he had Stella, Jasmine, and Spencer.

He turned his attention back to Spencer. "You're going west —to Crazy Horse. We're going east, then north to Mount Rushmore. Your closest route to us from Crazy Horse will be to continue north on 385."

"Right."

"If you are being followed, do not go that way."

"Okay." For the first time, Spencer's look of confidence wavered.

"Drive back to Custer and detour up Needles Highway. Lose the tail. Kill them if you can."

"Got it. But.... Who would tail me?"

John didn't honor that with an answer. Spencer could get tagged by any number of people. And would that be so bad? In some ways, it would rid John of one more loose end. The important thing was that the mission continue.

"You'll do great." He tossed the keys and Spencer caught them in his right hand. The kid had good reactions. "Don't get pulled over for speeding."

The grin returned. Ahh, the myriad ways that a toy could distract a person. It really was amazing.

Spencer got in the BMW and roared away.

John sank into the leather seat of the Voltaris and enjoyed the purr of the engine. The vehicle was like a symphony, a technological marvel, and a man's best fantasy all rolled into one.

No time to enjoy the present moment, though.

Twilight drew closer with every passing moment.

Time to get into position.

Kate reported back to the Mount Rushmore team at five p.m. Although she hadn't found any explosives or a single shred of proof that the AT had been on the property, Kate remained convinced that something would happen on this site within the next few hours. Her confidence and the call from Allison about the FlashLine ribbon found in trees along the Presidential Trail confirmed they were correct in their assessments of the danger to local tourists. The group from Crazy Horse agreed, and Ziolkowski made the decision to evacuate as many tourists as possible.

"A few can leave in their private vehicles." Morley Swanson stood in front of the whiteboard, jotting details and numbers as he spoke. "We estimate that on average approximately ten cars an hour leave, so between now and sunset we can lower this number..." He stood back and whacked the board with a pointer, emphasizing the size of the crowd visiting Crazy Horse.

It was an alarmingly large number.

"We can lower it by forty vehicles, which will be over forty people—probably closer to one hundred and sixty."

"Won't people arriving just replace those leaving?"

"Way ahead of you," Stoney Speidel said. "We're having an unexpected problem in the bathrooms. Owing to that as well as the already large numbers today, we won't be allowing any additional visitors. Signs are already up at the road as well as the toll booths."

"And we've put an apology out on social media," Talia said. She'd joined Tanner Larson earlier. "Even made a funny meme to go with it."

Kate thought it was good to see familiar faces—Talia, Leo, Tanner. Even Morley, Stoney, and Noah were starting to look like old friends. It made her feel this thing they were trying to accomplish might be possible. She wasn't standing in the breach between catastrophe and safety completely alone.

"We understand you don't want an empty parking lot because this AT group would simply move their attack." Speidel turned his attention back toward the whiteboard. "Our plan is to move additional tourists by using the bus that usually takes folks on a tour to see the work on the memorial. Instead, the bus will take them to a back entrance. We started ten minutes ago and believe we can evacuate all families as well as most other guests."

"Won't the AT realize what's happening?" Ziolkowski asked. "Won't they know what we're doing as this place becomes more and more deserted?"

"Only if they're already here," Kate said. "I don't think they are. I think they're at Mount Rushmore and what is going to happen here will happen remotely."

"Okay. That's good."

"Unless they have put surveillance throughout the visitor's center," Tanner said.

"They will. They have." Kate closed her eyes. She fought the urge to rub, but the itching suddenly felt unbearable. Stress? Lack of sleep? Pollen? Had an agent ever failed to perform because of pollen? She rubbed them, then stopped, knowing that would only make them feel worse.

"What can we do about that?" Swanson asked.

"Although my partners and I have remained off the grid, we brought a few cyber tools with us." She thought of the Faraday cage in the back of the Ford Bronco, the computers that were in hardened cases—effectively air-gapped, the state-of-the-art jammers.

"The techie side of my department has been working on a device called a SpectrumVeil. It's not ready for deployment yet, so no one else has one."

Speidel and Ziolkowski exchanged a look.

Speidel said what they were apparently both thinking. "But you have one."

"I do. I would not admit to that in a court of law, as these devices are rarely used in civilian scenarios. They dance on a fine line between a need to protect and regulatory restrictions."

"Sounds powerful," Tanner said.

"It is. A SpectrumVeil acts like a signal jammer, cellular jammer, GPS jammer and Wi-Fi/Bluetooth jammer all rolled into one. It effectively creates a bubble around a site. No information in. No information out."

"I've never heard of it," Speidel said. "And I thought I followed all of the tech R&D."

"There's probably more of tech research and development than one person could possibly follow." Kate felt an urge to do something, to be out there watching. But she also knew in the core of her being that these people needed to understand fully what they were getting into. "No one will be able to call out. You won't be able to reach your families or post on social media or check the weather. On the plus side, any surveillance devices they have planted will stop sending at the moment that we turn on the SpectrumVeil."

"We'll need to call out," Tanner said, addressing Morley Swanson. "We'll have to be able to call 9-1-1. We can evacuate all the guests, but how are we going to protect your workers? Or are they leaving too?"

"We'll keep a skeleton crew—people who know the risks and are willing to stay."

"How many is that?"

Speidel pulled a pad of paper toward him. "Twenty-eight."

Kate was impressed. She'd figured on far less. "I'm not comfortable putting those people in harm's way. I'm going to give you a list of likely locations for explosive devices, and I want you to communicate that list to your twenty-eight people."

"You got it."

"Do you have a landline here?"

"We do," Speidel said.

"Keep someone near that line at all times. First sign of trouble, place the call to 9-1-1. Not only will we want and need the help of emergency responders, but the AT will be monitoring the police channels. They'll be waiting for that call."

"And the SpectrumVeil?" Swanson asked.

"It's in my vehicle. I'll deploy it in the next twenty minutes."

"I'll assign someone to stand by the landline and be ready to make the call," Morley said.

"We also have an emergency fire team." Stoney Speidel was making notes on a pad of paper. "I'll update them on the target areas. They'll be as prepared as possible."

Tanner Larson added, "My people are trained emergency responders as well. They'll have first aid kits. We'll set up an emergency triage center back and away from the building—out of sight from the parking area."

The meeting broke up. Kate thanked each person for their sacrifice. When she spoke to Mr. Ziolkowski, tears stung her eyes and threatened to block her words.

"Take your time." He spoke softly, everything about his manner saying they had all the time in the world. They didn't. Kate understood how fast things were moving.

She looked away, blinked rapidly, pulled herself together. This man deserved to be looked in the eye. So she drew in a deep breath and did that. "What you have committed to doing, what you're willing to sacrifice for the good of this country, is nothing short of patriotic. I know you understand that this facility—all of this facility—may be reduced to a pile of rubble."

"Perhaps," he agreed. "But that is a worst-case scenario. I've listened clearly to everything you've said, Kate. The AT will be interested in maximum bang for their buck."

"Yes."

"It follows that the devices will be placed in the restaurant, the viewing veranda, and the gift shop. These are the busiest spots on the campus."

"They'll be destroyed."

"Probably, but buildings can be rebuilt. If the memorial itself suffered an attack, that would be much harder to accept. It represents decades of work. The facilities—we have the funds to rebuild. This is about more than buildings and memorials, though. What is being done to America, what this group has embraced as its mission, is deeply wrong."

"Yes."

"Sitting Bull once said *the life my people want is a life of freedom*. It's what we all want. And perhaps, today, after this is over, we'll be one step closer to achieving that life for everyone."

Tanner once again walked out of the building with her.

"What will you do?" he asked.

"Stay in the parking area. I think that John Howard, the head of this attack, will want eyes on. He'll send someone to confirm the attack actually happened."

"You know him pretty well."

"Too well."

"That must have been difficult."

"Yes."

Tanner looked as if he was waiting for her to say more, but Kate couldn't say more. She'd shared very little of her time in Middle Earth with her department-ordered therapist. As required by departmental policy, she'd relayed the facts of her undercover work, but she didn't possess the words to convey what it had done to her soul. So, she thanked him again and walked away.

At the Bronco, she retrieved the SpectrumVeil and carried it into a supply closet in the middle of the campus. After activating the jammer, she patrolled the site for the next two hours as the sun continued its descent and eventually disappeared behind the treeline. The light grew soft reminding her of the *gloaming*. She'd always loved that word. It brought to mind stories of hobbits and elves and fairy lights. Hard to believe that this twilight would bring danger and destruction instead of mystery and beauty.

She watched the bus go up and down the road that led to the actual construction site. Was one of John Howard's people watching? Would they notice the bus went up filled with people and came back empty? Kate was betting no. She thought she understood Howard's *Mode of Operation* pretty well. His *MO* had always been consistent. Use technology to beat technology, and only use people when technology could not be bought, bent, or manipulated to do the job.

Later she would wonder if it was God or fate or luck that had her standing at the back of the parking lot, standing near her vehicle, when the first explosion rocked the evening. As Ziolkowski had predicted, it appeared to be in the middle of the facility. Cries of alarm filled the evening. Those weren't rehearsed or shouted for the AT. They were authentic. Many people thought they were prepared for an impending attack, but few things could render a person ready for the deafening crack, the percussive boom, the shockwave that sent people, furniture, glass, and walls flying like shrapnel. That turned every object into a potential weapon.

Car alarms went off in those vehicles closest to the building. Flaming debris hit a motorcycle parked near the entrance, quickly engulfing it in fire. The acrid smell of smoke and charred debris rolled out from the building as, one after another, the sounds of another half dozen explosions filled the evening.

Kate wanted to run toward it.

The muscles in her calves began to quiver as her adrenaline spiked, and she had to force herself to remain still. Tanner's people would be working the site—as well as Swanson's. She needed to stay in position. And then she saw it. A black BMW sports car. It wasn't driving toward the scene. It wasn't speeding away. She grabbed her binoculars and centered in on the driver.

Spencer.

Spencer Parsons.

He paused in his drive-by to snap a few photos.

Kate hopped into the Bronco and peeled out after him. She got close, close enough that he looked in the rearview mirror, locked eyes with her, and grinned. Then he rammed the BMW's engine into a lower gear, shot out on the main road, and headed south toward Custer.

Chapter Fourteen

Kate floored the gas pedal on the Ford Bronco. There was a fifty-fifty chance that Spencer Parsons was leading her on a wild goose chase, intentionally hoping to draw her into a trap. But she was willing to walk into that trap if it meant stopping him.

Was there no limit to what he would do for one of John Howard's bonuses? She knew he wasn't a true believer. The only thing Spencer believed in was increasing the size of his bank account. She didn't know who she detested more—the fanatics who hoped to change the world or the greedy who stood by and profited from it falling apart.

As she drove in reckless pursuit, she imagined what was happening back at Crazy Horse.

Morley Swanson's people would be calling for help.

Stoney Speidel directing his emergency fire team.

Tanner Larson performing first aid on anyone injured—and she knew people had been injured. Explosions like that... They would be lucky if no one had been killed.

Kate knew she would struggle with what had happened there for a very long time. Could they have stopped it? Should they have stopped it? Should they have insisted everyone vacate the site? She also knew that right now, in this moment, she needed to completely focus on the mission at hand. What had happened at Crazy Horse was merely a decoy operation. It had worked too. She seemed to pass every emergency vehicle in the Black Hills area as they sped toward Crazy Horse. Which meant that the main event, the one John Howard had meticulously planned, was happening at Mount Rushmore.

Spencer drove the BMW M4 sports car like a madman. No doubt he was happy to have been given an assignment away from his keyboard, though really, that was the only place he excelled. He had a knack for hacking that even Kate found uncanny. Few people were satisfied with their natural talents, though. As she pushed the Bronco's engine, she realized he'd always enjoyed watching movies from the *Fast and Furious* franchise. No doubt he saw himself as Vin Diesel.

They sped recklessly down 385 toward Custer. There were no officers remotely interested in stopping them. Police cruisers flew by, all headed in the opposite direction. She and Spencer blew through Custer doing ninety miles an hour. She prayed the Bronco's engine would withstand the strain. Spencer made a tire-screaming left turn onto Highway 87.

Were they going to the Lodge?

Had John Howard figured out where they were staying?

What would be the point of going there now?

They passed the Needles Highway South Entrance Station, pushing their engines close to one hundred miles per hour. If any rangers were on duty, Kate didn't see them. Maybe everyone had been called to the situation at Crazy Horse. Maybe park rangers also served as emergency responders. The road split and Spencer didn't ease up on the pedal at all as he angled to the left. Kate's stomach sunk when she saw the sign cautioning larger vehicles to turn back.

The sign for Iron Creek Tunnel seemed to spell out her fate.

Width 9'
Height 12'

She could make that. Couldn't she? There was no way the Bronco was nine feet wide. Spencer bulleted through the opening and Kate tore after him. Prayed her hand would remain steady and her resolve wouldn't falter. Burst into the last of the day's sunshine cascading across the surrounding forest.

July in the Black Hills.

A thing of beauty.

Spencer must have slowed a little, no doubt hoping to watch her crash. She was close enough to see his gaze flick to the rearview mirror. Was he surprised? Amused? Afraid?

What was his plan here? During the entire time she'd worked for John Howard, she'd never known Spencer to have a plan. He worked on instinct, and his instinct seemed to be telling him to play with her like a cat with a mouse.

Screw that.

If there was one thing she knew she wasn't, it was a mouse. She'd survived working under John's steely gaze and Stella's insanity. She hadn't backed down even once. When her cover was blown, she hadn't panicked, and she would not do so now.

Analyze. Assess. Implement.

Use the eidetic memory that had been sometimes a curse and more often a blessing.

As the Bronco shot past evergreen trees, granite outcroppings, and empty parking areas, she did the calculations.

He was taking her toward the Needles Eye Tunnel. She'd seen a sign for that when they'd first entered and she passed another now.

Width 8'4"
Height 11'3"

Worse than Iron Creek—more narrow with less clearance.

Her vehicle was not a high-profile vehicle. She didn't know the width of the Bronco, but it definitely looked boxy. Certainly over six feet in width. No problem, then. She could make that almost as easily as she'd made the last one. If she didn't hesitate. Or waiver. At the speed they were going, the smallest swerve to the right or left would send her slamming into the granite walls of the tunnel.

Analyze. Assess. Implement.

They approached the tunnel on a road barely wide enough for two vehicles.

Road conditions were good—no recent rain.

His vehicle was new. Hers wasn't.

The Bronco had good tires, though, with reliable tread.

She wasn't a professional driver, but she was a damn sight better than that weaselly cyber bug skidding into a curve faster than any sensible person would. Spencer showed no sign of slowing down. Had he travelled this road before? Did he know something she didn't?

Nah. Spencer suffered from overconfidence. He'd always considered himself the smartest guy in the room—or, in this case, the smartest guy in the Black Hills.

Having committed herself to this course, she finished her assessment.

Most of the drop-offs they were passing had three-foot guardrails engineered to absorb impact and redirect the vehicle. It might redirect the sports cars given its low profile. The Bronco would soar right over it.

She calculated a minimal chance of inadvertent casualties. They had the place to themselves. Apparently, local tourists had opted for Crazy Horse or Mount Rushmore. Only two people remained with skin in this game—Spencer and Kate.

The landscape grew more rugged. Granite peaks jutted up from the ground, shadowing the road. She'd read that the tunnel they were nearing, the most narrow of the tunnels, was called Needles Eye because of its resemblance to the eye of a needle. She felt more like she was driving into the hand of God.

Granite spires towered to the right and the left as the road narrowed even more. Warning signs dotted the road side though she couldn't read them at the speed she was going. The directional signs were clear enough.

Turn left.

Winding road.

Hairpin curve.

Turn right.

The majestic scenery passed in a blur. The sound of the Bronco's engine receded. Kate had reached that spot in an op where everything distilled and focused down to a single point.

Them or her.

And she suddenly saw, clearly, what she would do.

If he slowed as he came out of the tunnel, she'd hit him. Ram him over the edge. Celebrate as he careened off into the void.

The world would be better off without the person driving that sports car.

She hadn't come to that conclusion easily. She wasn't the kind of person to give up on another human. But Spencer? He was enjoying this. He had enjoyed watching the explosions at Crazy Horse. She would not let him get away.

Everything in her conservative instincts told her to tap the brakes. Let off the gas. Live to fight another day.

She thought of the explosions.

The possible bodies.

The work of Korczak Ziolkowski threatened, the center created for visitors reduced to a pile of stone.

She was ready when the tunnel came into view. Spencer sped through it.

No other cars. No third-party victims.

She pushed the gas pedal to the floor.

Spencer didn't slow as he shot into the tunnel, then disappeared from sight. As Kate sped through the opening, the world went dark, but she didn't waver. One second passed, then two, and she saw light coming through the Needle's eye. The opening in front of her widened, and sunlight bounced off the sports car. Spencer had spun the BMW to a stop so that it was facing her. No doubt wanting a good view of her crash.

But Kate didn't crash into the tunnel's walls.

She didn't slow at all.

The Bronco hit the BMW head on, and she thought she saw his smug expression turn to surprise. Thought that in the split second before he disappeared over the edge of the cliff, she saw a flash of fear in his eyes.

The guardrail didn't have to redirect the impact because the sports car was now airborne, propelled by three thousand pounds of U.S. steel and a 302-cubic inch engine pushed to its limit, colliding with the finest of German automotive design.

Kinetic Energy (KE) = ½ mv2

It was a simple matter of physics. The BMW sailed over the railing, carrying Spencer Parsons with it. And though the collision had definitely slowed the Ford Bronco, it did not stop it. Kate pumped the brakes, attempted to steer the Bronco so that it would hit the guardrail at an angle, pressed her body against the seat and headrest. Nothing could have stopped the forward momentum of the Bronco. It slammed into the three foot high, carefully engineered guardrail.

The guardrail didn't hold.

Allison stood at the top of the amphitheater. If she'd been a cat, the hair on her neck would be standing up straight and her back would be arched. This was it. Whatever was going to happen was going to happen now.

Donovan had left the Mount Rushmore National Park for less than an hour and called Reid who would update the Director of Homeland Security, Kenneth Langston. Reid had agreed that the presence of FlashLine found in the trees on the property was confirmation an attack was imminent. He would send reinforcements, but with the current state of the union, it would take a little time. Shutting down the site was still a possibility, but everyone up the chain of command worried it would simply accelerate Howard's timeline. They needed to handle this very carefully.

For the last two hours, reports of the attack at Crazy Horse had filtered in. Some people left Mount Rushmore, though she was surprised at how many people stayed. They felt sympathy for their fellow Americans, but remained convinced that nothing would happen to them. The great American illusion. Or perhaps that was something felt worldwide—the idea that bad things happen over there, to someone else. Perhaps it was the only way that people were able to get up every day, pull on their pants, go to work, come home to the family. Maybe that routine required a bit of delusion—or positive thinking—whichever way you wanted to describe it.

That wasn't Allison's life, though. She'd expected bad things to happen since she was nine years old. Even now, she wanted to let her mind drift to Kate. Was she okay? Had she escaped unscathed? Was she simply remaining at her post?

The sun had set thirty minutes earlier, but darkness had yet to descend completely over the Black Hills. Donovan had left to take one more surveillance lap of the Presidential Trail. The amphitheater was full to bursting, and the Independence Day Fireworks show was about to begin.

Now.

It would happen now.

A pre-recorded voice told the visitors to "sit back and enjoy the celebration of their country's independence," then music began pouring from the speakers. Folks cheered and whistled.

Children waved flags. Teens looked up from their cell phones. It all made Allison's heart ache. This was America. These were true Americans, and she'd be damned if she was going to let the likes of John Howard harm a single one of them.

The rich tones of James Brown singing *Living in America* caused the few people still standing to find a seat, even when it meant pushing in between two strangers.

Allison had spent a summer undercover in central Texas, working in a fireworks booth. She knew what to expect from the show. She was confident she would know what didn't belong in the program. She scanned left, right, up, and down.

Donovan should have reached the far side of the Presidential Trail. She wished she could communicate with him. Wished she had a cell phone or a SAT phone or even a walkie-talkie. Fear flashed through her at the memory of him lying on the floor of the HVAC room aboard *Harmony of the Dreams*, blood pouring from his body. She pushed the memory away, sealed the fear in a box, focused on her job.

The music changed to Bruce Springsteen's *Born in the U.S.A.* The crowd oohed and awed as the fireworks began to razzle and dazzle, shoot and stream, arch higher and higher before draping over the monument like an umbrella. Willow Fireworks illuminated both the sky and the ground, giving the illusion of being caught under a willow tree's branches. Every eye was now turned toward the sky. Every eye, but Allison's.

She caught movement on the western part of the trail—the place where the invisible ribbon hung from a tree. In those few seconds, she saw the silhouette of two figures, each holding what looked like RPGs. Rocket-propelled grenades? They wouldn't...

As she watched, both pointed their shoulder-fired weapons toward the sky and fired. At least she thought they must have fired, but there was no explosion, no violent shaking, no screams of terror. Had they fired the equivalent of a blank to check their trajectory? But that wouldn't have been necessary given the FlashLine.

The willow fireworks changed to comets, and the area went momentarily dark, but they were followed by Aerial Shells carrying an explosion of color and light.

Her heart raced and sweat dripped down the back of her neck. She wanted to sprint into action, and she knew she needed to stay in place, to watch, to understand what was happening. She saw the same two figures next to the monolith. They'd apparently rearmed their weapons and were now pointing them toward the left and the right of the amphitheater.

This was it.

She shouted, "Get down," and threw herself over a small child seated a few feet in front of her. The explosions hit to the left and right of the amphitheater, no doubt falling somewhere along the darkened trail, causing the ground to shake.

Some thought it was another aspect of the show.

A few looked around in concern.

The parents of the child that Allison had tried to protect pulled the crying girl into their arms.

Allison didn't bother explaining herself. Instead, she strode toward the park director. Moss had seen what she had and was attempting to talk into his cell phone, which, of course, wasn't working. He turned to her, face pale, eyes wide.

"Get them inside."

"In there?"

"Your cell phones won't work. The first two blasts were EMPs. The second two were actual explosions. Unlock the doors and have your people move everyone as far into the facility as possible. Go. Now!"

Though he looked at her as if she'd lost her mind, he quickly recovered and began shouting for personnel to unlock the facility.

She might have expected a stampede, and maybe under other circumstances there would have been. At the moment, Lee Greenwood was singing "God Bless the U.S.A." That was a piece of luck. Whether consciously or not, people responded to that song, to those words. Or maybe some still thought this was part of the show. They helped one another, moved in an orderly fashion, followed directions.

That wouldn't last.

But it might at least get them inside.

"Who's attacking us?" She'd been unaware that Grey Hopkins, one of the National Park rangers had moved next to her.

"The AT, and I don't have time to explain any more than that. Get them inside."

"If they hit the building..."

"They might, but they're still safer in there than they will be out here."

He nodded once, curtly, before turning and hurrying to help someone pushing a wheelchair. A few people tried to head toward the parking area, but a parks worker cut them off and insisted they turn around. He might not have been successful in persuading them, but at that moment another RPG hit the parking area, causing a loud explosion, the beep of car alarms, and screams from the folks who had been headed in that direction. They turned and ran into the building.

The amphitheater was now empty. She understood it was what John Howard wanted. At this point, he was calling all the shots. Let him believe they were meekly doing what his diabolical plans had predicted they would do. If he was overly confident, he'd be more likely to make a mistake. With one last look toward the trail, toward where Donovan had to be, Allison turned and jogged into the facility.

Clarence Moss and Grey Hopkins were standing at the double doors, both attempting to calm groups of people who were shouting for answers. She pulled them away, lowered her voice.

"Lock the doors," Allison said. "We don't want the people out there coming in."

"Won't they just bomb their way in?"

"If they were going to do that, they already would have. The AT's show has just started. There's something he wants everyone to see."

At that moment, the lights blinked and a voice, what she recognized as John Howard's voice, came over the sound system.

"You have been misled. You have been lied to, but today is the day of your independence. As you now realize, your cellular devices no longer work."

He'd somehow tapped into the security system and used the cameras throughout the facility to project pictures of the most popular digital "intrusions" into their lives.

Allison cringed at his voice while she watched what was playing out, looking for clues, analyzing what she saw—the plethora of images appearing on the screens.

Cell phones and laptops.

Streaming platforms and social media.

Electric vehicles and autonomous robotic vacuum cleaners.

Satellite arrays.

"You believe these things have made your life easier, but the same technology ... the same government ... that has allowed you these toys has subverted newer developments in robotics and artificial intelligence to control and enslave you."

The images grew more sinister. Drone attacks on foreign lands. Patrol robots. Augmented K9 units. Vast data centers.

"It's time that we turn this country around."

The image switched to a live shot, though it was framed by a border of the most popular tech devices. John Howard appeared to be standing at the base of the monument. It looked to Allison like he was filming live on the Presidential Trail. Was he insane enough to broadcast his location? If so, that could only mean two things.

One—he didn't think anyone would survive long enough to capture him.

Two—he wasn't planning on sticking around for long.

"Our country is infected, but you—you have been chosen. You will be the emissaries of a new America. You will be the ones that spread the message of freedom."

John Howard, his voice, and the frame of images disappeared. It its place, a simple countdown clock was projected.

0:20:00
0:19:59
0:19:58

Allison's mind picked out the words he'd emphasized.

Infected. Chosen. Emissaries. Spread.

Clarence Moss was still attempting to find a phone that worked as his employees dealt with the assembled tourists.

Grey Hopkins pushed through the crowd and jerked his head to an alcove. Once there, he said, "These people will not sit here for the next twenty minutes."

"Agreed."

"What's your plan?"

Allison was still thinking about Howard's last message, what he would probably label his *call to action*. She had no doubt that he'd chosen each word carefully.

Infected. Chosen. Emissaries. Spread.

"I need to see your HVAC room."

"I can take you."

"No. You need to speak to these people."

His gaze met hers, and she saw in his eyes not surprise or panic, but a calm acceptance. Grey Hopkins had seen this type of horror again and again, or at least something equally tragic. His expression said that and more. He understood what was at stake.

Allison knew the people assembled would listen to him.

He pulled his key ring off his belt, found the correct key, pushed it into her hands, and gave her directions to the room where the building's air conditioning, heating, and air filtration systems were kept.

As she sprinted down the hall, as she remembered the anthrax that had been released on board the cruise ship, she heard his voice behind her speaking to the tourists. His tone was strong, confident, unafraid. She couldn't make out his words. She didn't need to. He would take care of the people gathered there. She had less than eighteen minutes to stop a bioweapon from being exploded within the facility. The alternative was to move everyone back outside, where she suspected Howard's goons waited with their automatic weapons.

Chapter Fifteen

Allison took one look at the dispersal device and knew she wouldn't be able to disarm it. The canister had been welded to the HVAC system and was accompanied by its own propellant system. Turning off the HVAC system wouldn't work. The air propulsion unit that John had so carefully installed would simply take over the job of propelling his poison through the building's air ducts.

She sprinted back to the theater room where all the tourists were amassed, slowing only to take a look at the time projected on the wall.

0:12:47
0:12:46

She skidded to a stop next to Grey Hopkins. Clarence Moss was nowhere to be seen.

"We have to get them outside."

"I just convinced them to stay inside."

Allison pushed her hand into her side where a cramp felt like a knife pushed into her organs. "I can't stop it."

His eyes met hers. He didn't ask *are you sure* or *stop what* or *isn't there another way*. He took the keys from her hand, again selected one, and handed it back. "This will unlock the outside doors."

"Get them as far away from the building as you can. I don't know what he used, but it'll be nasty." She ran toward the front door, nearly fumbled the keys, caught them, found the one Grey had handed her, slipped it into the keyhole, and pushed out into the cool night air.

She could still smell the acrid smoke from the rockets that had been fired earlier. Had it only been a few minutes ago? She didn't pause to assess the damage. Instead, she hit the trail at an all-out run determined to find and stop John Howard before he escaped. She went willingly into the darkness, passing the Youth Exploration Area, then the Abraham Lincoln overlook, George Washington, the Talus Terrace. A part of her mind wanted to linger on the fact that she'd passed these spots on the trail with Donovan earlier that day

Was he still alive?

Why hadn't he shown up when the RPGs went off?

Where was he now?

John Howard had taken her father from her. Had he also taken her best friend? Had he, again, taken the man she loved?

Allison didn't stop until she reached the curve in the trail that led to the best view of the monument. The place where tourists paused to take family pictures.

She stopped, pressed her back against a tree, and slowed her heart rate. She couldn't banish the part of herself that remembered being a young girl, wearing a Dora Explorer t-shirt, back pressed against a giant redwood tree as her father was killed. That horrific experience would follow her until her last breath. She didn't want to forget. She wanted to channel it. She wanted to use all of her anger and resentment and loss and fear against the man waiting for her around the corner.

She pulled in one more deep breath, checked her weapon, and peered around the corner.

A woman she didn't know, a woman who couldn't possibly have been Stella Gonzalez, stood with a phone held out toward John Howard. A portable flood light sat on the ground, pointed toward him, no doubt to ensure a better live feed.

Allison stepped out into the open, her firearm firmly gripped between both hands, a strange calm encasing her emotions.

"Stop recording. Both of you—hands in the air."

Allison expected them to comply, though a part of her hoped they wouldn't.

A part of her wanted to kill this man.

She couldn't stop what was about to happen back at the visitor's center, but she could stop this psychopath from ever hurting anyone again.

What she did not expect was to feel the cold barrel of a gun pressed against the back of her neck.

"Not so fast. Eject the magazine. Nice and slow. My fingers twitch sometimes. You wouldn't want me to blow your head off."

The younger woman had turned toward them, still holding the phone, still recording.

"Smile, Allison. You're on social media and streaming on every wireless feed in the country."

It was an older woman standing behind her. The way she spoke reminded Allison of a snake slithering across the ground.

"You're being livestreamed across the country. Hands behind your back now."

She wasn't about to be handcuffed by an octogenarian.

She turned, elbow pulled back, ready to deliver a lethal blow, and as quick as a viper strikes, the woman shot her in the leg. Allison felt white hot pain. Pain so intense, she wondered how the human body could withstand it. Familiar pain. It poured through her body. She tried to hold herself up, but gravity and anatomy prevented that. She dropped to the trail like a stone tossed from a three story building.

Allison turned on her stomach and attempted to crawl into the darkness, which her assailant seemed to find extremely funny.

"Just like her daddy. Isn't she, John?"

The woman walked toward her, used a designer shoe to push her over onto her back, and held her there. How was it that Allison wasn't able to push that foot away? This woman was at least eighty, and she looked as if she weighed less than a hundred pounds. She pulled a cloth out of her pocket, then a small bottle. After donning a mask, she shook something from the bottle onto the cloth. The sweet, fruity smell reached Allison. She attempted to turn on her stomach again, to flee, but her leg was like an impossibly heavy weight.

"I'm Stella. You don't know me yet, but you will." The woman once more held the pistol in her right hand, the chloroform rag in her left. "Be still now, or you'll force me to shoot you again."

Allison's training took over.

When all else fails, survive to fight another day.

Instead of struggling, she focused on memorizing the woman's face. She stared into her eyes, dark orbs that frightened her more than the gun or the sedative that was now being pressed to her nose and mouth. Her muscles relaxed. The pain in her leg became nothing. And then, all was lost as she fell into the deep well of unconsciousness.

The climb up and out of the ravine was a difficult one. By the time Kate reached the top, her hands were scratched and bleeding, though not as badly as her left arm. The large knot on her forehead throbbed. For better or worse, the Bronco had not been equipped with airbags, so at least she didn't have to deal with powder burns. Miraculously, the seatbelt had held.

She turned to look at the guardrail.

The Bronco had taken out a five-foot section, but the guardrail had done what it was designed to do—slow her impact, change her trajectory. Instead of following Spencer to his death, her vehicle had tumbled, ricocheted, bounced, and at last came to rest against a large evergreen tree.

She'd passed out at least once, but finally had cut herself free of the seatbelt, exited through the shattered windshield, climbed over the hood of the Bronco, then struggled her way, carefully, painfully up and out of the ravine. By the time she reached the road, darkness had settled across the Black Hills along with an unnatural quiet.

She once more did a quick assessment.

No broken bones.

She might need some stitches, but the strip of shirt she'd wrapped around her left arm was at least slowing the bleeding.

Her firearm was still in her ankle holster.

If she could just find her phone.

She had no phone.

But she possibly had a concussion because she had definitely forgotten she was now stranded in the middle of the Black Hills with no way to call for help.

Had the attack at Mount Rushmore already happened?

Were her friends alive or dead?

And what of John Howard?

She started walking back toward the entrance they'd blown through. Entered the tunnel and came out the other side. She took the terrifying journey of a few hours before in reverse. One foot in front of the other. Enough starlight to help her see the road. No traffic. One mile. Then two. She tried to remember how many miles they'd driven after entering Needles Highway, then gave up. She'd walk until she reached the Visitor Entrance. If no one was there, she'd walk to Custer. She'd acquire a vehicle. Then she'd go to Rushmore. She'd rejoin her team. She'd find Donovan and Allison, and together they'd see this thing through to the end.

Headlights coming around a curve startled her, and she nearly stumbled. The driver slowed, then stopped, slipped the compact car's engine into neutral, and opened the door.

Could this possibly be another of John Howard's crew?

She calculated how long it would take her to pull her Sig Sauer. Knelt as if to tie her shoe. Closed her palm around the handle of the P320.

"You okay, miss?"

The kid's voice, which hadn't finished changing yet, cracked on the word miss. He must have been closing in on six feet tall. She wondered how he managed to fit behind the wheel of the compact.

He stopped a respectful five feet from her.

The headlights of his vehicle showed he was wearing hiking pants, hiking shoes, and a matching hiking shirt. Plus a hiker's hat on his head. All were top of the line but also well used. He was the real thing.

"You're bleeding. Say, were you in that crash? My buddies and I saw it from the hiking trail we were on. They took the north side of the road, and I took the south. We tried 9-1-1, but only got a busy signal which seemed pretty strange."

Kate let out a sigh, offered what she hoped was a small laugh and stood—or tried to stand. Her left ankle wobbled, and she almost went down. He was at her side before she realized he was moving toward her. She felt that shift in time again, as if she'd lost a few seconds.

Was that what a concussion did to you? Caused time to slip? It was disorienting and more than a little scary. She'd do her best to protect her head from this point forward.

"Say. We need to get you to town. No hospital there, but there's a clinic that's open nights, weekends, even holidays."

"Did you say you saw a crash?"

"Saw something. Must have been a crash. Looked like a fire-ball in the ravine behind you. The one past the tunnel."

She hadn't realized until that moment that a small part of her had worried Spencer might have survived.

He hadn't.

Spencer Parsons would never hack into a computer system again. He wouldn't be the author of destruction. He wouldn't be John Howard's minion.

They'd reached the compact car. She rested against the hood as the kid reached into the vehicle and pulled out a steel water bottle, unscrewed the lid, handed it to her. And suddenly Kate felt a thirst so powerful she feared she would pass out.

She took the bottle in shaking hands, drank greedily, then more slowly, and finally handed it back to him. "What's your name?"

"Brody. Brody Jones."

"Nice to meet you, Brody. My name is Kate Ballou." And how wonderful that was, to use her actual name again. She wasn't Kate Jackson, the undercover agent working for John Howard. Or Kate Johnson, as her fake ID declared. She was Kate Ballou, born in Shreveport, Louisiana, trained at Quantico, and a member of the Joint Cyber Task Force.

Brody was nodding and smiling and hovering a bit, as if he might need to catch her again. His smile turned to puzzlement when she said, "I'm going to need to borrow your car."

Chapter Sixteen

Kate arrived at Mount Rushmore to find the most chaotic scene of her career. Choppers were landing and lifting off. A triage center had been set up a hundred yards from the actual visitor center complex. Ambulances filled the area between the complex and the triage center. It looked as if several bombs had gone off at the site, and government personnel in biohazard suits were moving in and out of the main visitor center.

Tourists were everywhere.

Huddled in groups, voices low, expressions indicating they were still in shock. Many had emergency mylar blankets wrapped around their shoulders, though it was a relatively warm evening. Those with the most severe injuries had apparently already received first aid, and paramedics were attending to minor injuries as she flashed her phony ID and walked past them.

A little frightening that—how easy it was to access the site with a fake ID. But then the damage had already been done. No one was expecting the perpetrators to come back. Would they come back? She paused and scanned the area, looking for anyone familiar, anyone from the AT. Not John Howard. Not Stella

Gonzalez. Maybe one of the lesser minions. But the crowd was too large, and she didn't see anyone that appeared to be a threat.

She was heading to look for whomever was in charge of this still very active scene when she saw a large Black man walking through the crowd, walking toward her.

Donovan didn't ask if she needed a hug. He wrapped his arms around her and rested his chin on the top of her head, breathing in and out, and providing them both—for the briefest of moments—a refuge. Finally, he held her at arm's length. "You need a medic?"

"No. I'm fine."

He touched the goose egg on her forehead, and she flinched away.

"I need you, Kate. I need you to help me go after Allison."

"Go after her? What do you mean, go after her?"

But Donovan was already turning toward a medic. "Can we get a hand over here?"

Kate started to argue, but he stopped her with a quick shake of his head. "You and me. We have to rescue Allison. If it's anyone else, if John Howard sees anyone else, he'll kill her."

Kate had been through a lot in the last twelve hours, but when Donovan said those last three words, she felt as if she'd been smacked in the head with a baseball bat.

He'll kill her.

And in that moment, something rose in her, something akin to what she'd experience when she'd smashed the Bronco into Spencer's BMW, but stronger. The feeling was more than rage. It was an unwavering commitment to save her friend. It was a resolve so deep that she felt as if it sprang from her soul.

"Let's meet at the Bronco. You parked it over there?" Donovan nodded past the emergency vehicles.

"Not exactly."

"Where?"

"The Bronco's gone."

His eyes went to the knot on her head, the makeshift bandage around her arm, the torn clothes. He nodded and wiped a large hand across his face. "I'll find another vehicle. The van was crushed when the AT's grenade hit the parking garage, but I'll requisition us another ride."

"I have a vehicle."

Donovan's trademark smile spread across his face. "Of course you do. Where's it parked?"

"Southeast side of the parking garage."

"Let the medic clean you up. Meet me there in fifteen." He squeezed her good arm one more time, then disappeared into the crowd.

The young woman wearing an EMT patch on her jacket waved her over. Kate went and sat in the back of the ambulance, though it was absolutely the last thing she wanted to be doing at this moment.

He'll kill her.

Only over Kate's cold, dead body because if she was alive she would find a way to stop him.

She sat still as the medic cleaned her cuts and reapplied bandages. She even answered all of the woman's questions.

Yes, the bump hurt. No, she wasn't seeing double. Yes, she'd lost a bit of blood. Butterfly stitches would be fine for now. She didn't think anything was broken. The ankle was already feeling better.

A bit of a lie on that last one.

Which didn't matter because the woman wasn't buying it.

She uncapped a bottle of water and handed it to her with three Advil. "This will help for a little while, but you need to get that ankle x-rayed."

"Will do."

The woman had been completely professional until the moment that Kate stood, flinched, then quickly covered up the slip with a smile. She was prepared to leave, ready to do her job.

"I was at Crazy Horse," the paramedic said. "Earlier tonight, when the bombs went off."

"Me too."

"Now this."

"Yeah. Now this. What's with the biohazard suits?"

"I don't really know. I've heard smallpox. Possibly Ebola. Some sort of bioweapon that was delivered via the HVAC system. Everyone was sheltering inside there, inside the building because of the grenades that were going off, and then suddenly they were told to evacuate and go back outside."

"Told by whom?"

"One of the park rangers, who said he was given those direction by a woman."

Allison. Allison had saved these people.

"Are you going after them ... after whoever did this?"

Their eyes met, and Kate realized Allison wasn't the only reason she would find and kill John Howard before the night was over. This woman was also a reason. All of the emergency responders. All the victims. "Yeah. I am."

"I thought so. Godspeed."

"Thank you."

The medic turned to her next patient and Kate limped off to find Donovan. Someone had set up even more floodlights around the site. The glaring lights somehow made the scene appear even more nightmarish. A team wearing jackets with JCTF printed in bold letters across their backs was disembarking from one of the copters. Donovan was updating the team lead who gave Kate a once over when she walked up.

"Good to see you in one piece, Ballou."

"More or less." She shook Jackson Warren's hand, then accepted the credentials package and SAT phone he handed her.

"Gifts from the boss," he said. "Do you need a firearm?"

"Still have my Sig," Kate assured him.

But Donovan was way ahead of her. "We could use a Stoner Rifle."

Warren's eyebrow shot up, but he didn't question Donovan about it. The situation was fluid, and it was plain that Donovan and Kate weren't finished with this evening or this fight. "Sure. Always carry two in the chopper."

He barked an order to someone on his team, then turned back to Kate and Donovan. "Can we provide back-up?"

Donovan wiggled his SAT phone. "We'll call if we need you."

"Fair enough. Then I'm off to see if the AT left a cyber trail, or perhaps some good old-fashioned fingerprints."

"Good luck," Donovan said.

"Yeah. You two get some rest." He put a special emphasis on the word *rest* as another team member handed Donovan the rifle. "Remember to call Langston. He wants to hear from you directly."

"Got it," Kate said.

Donovan followed her through the triage area and out the other side. They circled around to where she'd left the Dodge Neon.

"This is it? I'm not sure I'll even fit in this car, Kate."

"Didn't have the luxury of being picky as I was walking back from Needles Highway."

"You need to update me on that."

"And you need to tell me why Jackson handed you a sniper rifle, but pretended to believe we're going to rest." She emphasized the last word, which she found insulting. As if—

"Fair enough. We have an hour's drive ahead of us. Plenty of time to debrief each other."

"Deal. You want to drive?"

"I want to *try* to drive, if I can fit into this clown car."

"I'll drive."

"You're the one with a messed up ankle and a concussion. Don't think I didn't notice."

"A girl can hope."

He tossed her a smile, placed the rifle in the back seat, and squeezed behind the wheel by pushing the seat all the way back, though it was still a tight fit. Donovan didn't complain, though. He also didn't immediately start the car.

"I want to show you something before we start out." He pulled out his phone and pressed play on a video of John Howard, standing in front of the Mount Rushmore National Memorial. In the middle of his saying something about "freeing America," the person filming turned, and the screen filled with the image of Allison, clasping her weapon in both hands, pointing it toward John.

She looked fearless, completely in control, and unaware of the woman moving closer behind her.

"That's Stella—Stella Gonzalez."

"Yeah."

She watched in horror as Stella attempted to disarm Allison. When Allison refused to comply, Kate almost closed her eyes. She knew what would come next. Knew the ruthlessness and cruelty of John's financier. Though she expected it, Kate jerked at the sound of the gunshot, watched Allison drop to the ground, attempt to crawl away, and be sedated.

With hands that shook more than a little, she reached for the phone, and played the entire clip again. "So, he has her."

"He does."

"And you have this tape because..."

"Because he continued to livestream it. Everyone connected to the internet in this country, maybe in the world, saw what happened."

"He's using her as an example."

"Possibly. Or possibly someone is settling an old grudge. Maybe Stella is the one who killed Allison's father." Donovan let that sink in, then added, "There's something else."

She waited.

"Guy named Grey Hopkins. He's former military. He's going with us."

"Why?"

"Because we can't do this alone. He offered, and he has experience with the SR-25. More than you or I do."

"And you trust him?"

Donovan blew out a breath, then turned to meet her gaze. "I

do trust him. He followed Allison's orders and helped move the visitors to safety. I have that from more than half a dozen witnesses. He put his own life on the line to make sure everyone got out before the bioweapon went off. Also, he knows the area. Knows this area. Knows Spearfish Canyon."

"That's where we're going?"

"Yeah."

"There's something else."

"There is," Donovan admitted. "We have to throw John Howard off his game. He's calling all the shots at this point. We have to be willing to take a risk if we're going to get Allison back alive."

"Okay. I'm in. Whatever it takes."

He adjusted the mirrors, started the vehicle, and maneuvered to the outer perimeter of the blockaded area. Lots of vehicles trying to get in. Very few trying to get out. One guy standing on their side of the barricades—waiting.

Grey Hopkins was probably five foot eleven, tanned, fit. He wore a National Park Ranger uniform. When Donovan stopped the car and jumped out, Grey folded himself into the backseat without a word, moving the rifle over as he did so. Donovan flashed his creds at the local police, and they were waved through the final barricade.

Kate glanced into the back seat. The tiny back window was now completely obscured by Grey's head.

"Grey Hopkins," he said, buckling himself into the middle portion of the back seat, which was barely large enough for three small children.

"Kate. Kate Ballou."

Grey offered nothing else, but Kate felt his eyes assessing her.

"Can you explain to me what happened back there?" Kate asked.

"I can tell you what I saw."

Donovan floored the accelerator, which didn't have quite the effect one might have hoped for. "First, let's talk about where we're headed."

"You said Spearfish. Why there?"

Instead of answering, he handed her a piece of paper with his name—his correct name, which no one should have known—scrawled on the outside. She touched the dome light and unfolded the single sheet. Grey leaned forward so that he could read it over her shoulder.

> *We have her.*
>
> *Spearfish Canyon.*
>
> *Only you and Kate.*
>
> *0200 hours*
>
> *44.338140, -103.964640*

"I already plugged those coordinates into my phone," Grey said. "It's Roughlock Falls. Pretty remote spot."

"Speaking of phones..." Kate studied Donovan. "Why are we embracing technology again? Aren't we worried the AT can track us? Why are we taking that risk?"

"Couple of reasons," Donovan said. "First, we know that somehow the AT is hacking into encrypted phones, but it's not something that John Howard can do with the snap of a finger. His capabilities are going to be limited given that he's on the run."

"Maybe," Kate said. Was that true? She'd always worked in the lair. She'd never taken part in an active op out in the real world—not on the AT's side of things. John had been forced to move his operational center from Montana. Had he had time to rebuild his entire facility? She didn't know, and she couldn't accurately guess what their mobile capabilities were.

"Second reason is pretty simple. The AT has no way of knowing which phones were given to us. Warren had a box of them. Told me to call into JCTF with my number when I had a chance."

"Uh-huh."

Grey again leaned forward. "Cell reception isn't great up in these canyons. I suspect SAT phones won't work as well as we'd like either."

"You say that like it's an advantage."

"It is, because he won't be able to track us."

Kate felt her head clearing. Her adrenaline had surged, dipped, then surged again over the last few hours. She finally felt as if her prefrontal cortex was in control once more.

"Though, it's also a disadvantage because we can't count on them working." Donovan shrugged. "We'll deal with that when and if we need to."

"Obviously, our phones will take us to these coordinates." Kate squirmed around in her seat and made eye contact with Grey. He didn't glance away, and she gave him points for that. "How familiar are you with the terrain?"

"Hiked it a few times, most recently in the spring. Like I said, it's remote, but accessible. On a holiday weekend like this, most people congregate together. This John Howard guy, or the AT, or whoever it is we're chasing, picked an excellent spot if they wanted a showdown."

Kate's thoughts flashed back to the cold and calculating ways of John Howard. "Make no mistake, he does not want a showdown. He wants to win—decisively. He won't play fair, and he won't follow any rules. For all we know, he's already killed Allison."

"We're going to operate on the assumption that he hasn't." Donovan's voice wasn't a growl. Not exactly. "That's what she'd do if he had one of us."

"Right."

"Right."

"Walk me through what happened back at Mount Rushmore," Kate said.

Grey gave a two-sentence explanation of his history, his familiarity with the SR-25. Then he told about the RPGs, the flight into the building, John Howard's message projected across the entire network, Allison's attempt to stop the attack and—when she couldn't—her insistence that they move everyone back outside. "Then she just took off west, on the Presidential Trail."

"I somehow missed her." Donovan picked up the story. "I was reconnoitering the trail, and had made it nearly back to the visitor center when I heard the first explosions. Part of that debris blocked my path."

He stopped, stared out the window, tightened his hands on the wheel. "Took me too long to clear a way through."

Donovan turned over his hand and, by the light of the dash, stared at the palm that was cut and bruised—first one hand, then the other. "By the time I did make it back, Allison was already gone, people were streaming out to the parking area, more grenades were landing and then the bioweapon went off."

"Did everyone get out in time?"

"Everyone except my boss," Grey said. "He went back into his office to grab something. I don't know what. What would have been worth dying for?"

"In most instances, people who walk back into danger do so because they refuse to recognize the threat." Kate steepled her fingers together. Something was missing. Something that hadn't been explained.

Donovan got there first. "How did John Howard know we were here? How did he know I was here? And Allison? And even you?"

That was it.

That was the thing that still didn't make sense. No one even suggested that Allison had offered up the information.

They'd been so careful. Avoided every type of technology. How had he done it?

Donovan said, "The message with my name on it was given to

a first responder, who was told it was urgent and to give it to the person in charge."

"Since my boss, Clarence Moss, couldn't be found it was brought to me." Grey shrugged. "I wasn't exactly in charge, but close enough, I guess."

"But Donovan, no one knew your real name. How did Grey know to give it to you?" Kate resisted an urge to chew on her thumbnail, or touch the SIG in her ankle holster. All of this speculation was making her nervous.

"John Howard knew that once the attack had begun, we would revert to our true identities, which I did. When I finally made it past the debris on the trail, I introduced myself as Donovan Steele, a member of the JCTF, and I asked to speak to the person in charge."

"Which was how you found me." Grey sat back. "How did this John Howard know you were there, though?"

"Someone on the inside of your group, maybe." Kate again turned in her seat. "Someone who had been bought off and was on the lookout for us. Donovan doesn't exactly need a picture on his wanted poster."

"True," Donovan murmured. "Has anyone on your staff been acting odd? Nervous maybe?"

"No. I would say Rhonda Franklin, but actually, she died last night."

Kate locked eyes with Donovan, then turned back to Dan. "How did she die?"

"Car accident."

"Okay—" She drew out the word as a shiver tiptoed down her spine. "And what did she drive?"

"One of those EVs. She always seemed to be short on money, but she was proud of that electric vehicle."

And then it all made sense. The last piece of the puzzle fell into place, making for a dark and macabre scene. Kate explained it to them succinctly. Find someone in financial need. Present what you want—in this case to be on the lookout for one rather large black man who looked like an NFL player and a small, wiry woman with a mess of brown curls. Possibly together. How hard would it be? As for Kate, they would have had a picture of her from the days she worked undercover in the AT.

Grey was catching up quickly. "So, did John Howard bribe her? Or kill her?"

"Both," they said in unison.

Which only left Kate's part of the story to share. Spencer Parsons, how she'd spotted him at Crazy Horse after the explosions, her pursuit of him through Needles Highway, and his death.

"Wow," Donovan said.

Grey was leaning so far forward, he was practically sitting between them. "Weren't you afraid of going over the edge?"

"In the moment, no. I was more afraid of Spencer getting away. Of him doing what he did at Crazy Horse and Mount Rushmore again and again."

They all spent a moment staring out at the road which was eerily empty of traffic. Finally, everyone had decided to stay home —John Howard's message received, loud and clear. They drove past the sign welcoming them to Rapid City. This place, too, looked oddly devoid of traffic. No doubt, word was out about the attacks. People would be home, gathered around their loved ones —glued to their televisions and cell phones.

Donovan switched to the fast lane and once again tried to punch the accelerator of the compact car. "Spencer must have called John, maybe when he first spotted you at Crazy Horse. He told John that you were in the area, but how did John know you survived the crash?"

"He didn't. He doesn't. He doesn't even know about the crash, and he doesn't know that Spencer is dead. He might suspect it, since Spencer won't have checked in. Even if Spencer called it in, without confirmation he can't know where I am. For all John knows, I simply gave him the slip."

"Which brings us back to the note."

"Yeah, the note."

"He's guessing."

"Or following his instincts, which have always been very good. It's the reason he's still alive."

Grey leaned forward. "Tell me you guys have a plan."

Then he sat back and listened, interrupting only on the most crucial points, as they told him how the three of them would rescue Allison Quinn, and once and for all bring an end to the Anarchists for Tomorrow.

Chapter Seventeen

John Howard was not pleased. In fact, he had an overpowering urge to break something. This should be the shining moment of the AT movement. Stella should be celebrating, and John should feel some measure of vindication for the death of his wife and daughter. None of those things were happening. Why? Because none of the indicators he'd expected to see were appearing.

No mass casualties at the area hospitals.

No Marshall Law declared by the governor.

No notice that the President would address the nation.

Of course, there was coverage on the news, chat boards, and social media sites. But the government was not responding to the present threat with the appropriate amount of concern. It was almost as if they didn't realize that hundreds had been killed, that two of the nation's symbols of democracy had been destroyed, and that a biohazard was spreading among the population.

Unless it wasn't. He hadn't heard from the men who fired the RPGs. They'd been told that both shots fired would be EMP blasts. John hadn't wanted them to get cold feet at the last minute. For one reason or another, they'd vanished into the night.

While the news showed government agents in hazmat suits,

the hospitals were not being flooded with patients. Was it possible that someone had warned them? Why weren't there massive casualties at Crazy Horse? And where was Spencer Parsons?

"Tell me again why I can't kill her?"

John closed his eyes, breathed in deeply, then out slowly as his on-line meditation instructor had taught him. It didn't help. He looked over at Allison Quinn, still unconscious, lying on the only bed in the cabin. She might bleed through the bandages and stain the worn quilt, but he didn't care. He didn't plan on sleeping on the bed. He certainly didn't plan on spending the night there. Looking at her, he thought of all the trouble she'd caused him. He wouldn't mind putting a bullet through her himself, but he had a little more control over his emotions than Stella Gonzalez.

"She's bait, Stella. Why can't you understand that?"

"Donovan and Jackson don't even know if she's alive or dead. We don't even know if they received the note."

"They'll be here. Trust me. Those three are thick as thieves."

"I don't care about Donovan Steele. Kate was your mistake, and you can clean it up. But Arthur Quinn ruined my life. He stole from me."

"And you killed him for it."

"I killed him. Yes, I did. That isn't enough though because now this ... this ... this pitiful excuse for an agent, for a woman, is within ten feet of me, and she's still breathing. I don't want her to still be breathing, John."

Her eyes had taken on a demented look. Stella Gonzalez was losing it. He'd known it would happen, eventually. He'd simply hoped to be far, far away when it did.

"You saw the wisdom of not killing her back at Mount Rushmore—"

"I should have killed her then," she screamed, then lurched for the handgun resting on the small Formica top table.

John beat her to it, felt her hands clawing at his, and wondered again if she was crazy enough to have painted poisonous fingernail polish on her nails. He pushed her away, causing her to stumble backwards, and then a look of wild fury came over her face. He understood she meant to come after him.

Should he shoot her?

"I have something." Jasmine didn't look up from her laptop. Jasmine wasn't big on making eye contact. It was something that John found both endearing and a bit irritating.

"Tell us," he said, putting the handgun into the waistband of his pants and stepping to the opposite side of the computer to create distance between himself and Stella.

Stella straightened her clothes, looked around as if she might find a drink waiting for her, scowled at John, then moved closer so that she could see Jasmine's computer screen.

"I wrote a program to isolate any cell phones travelling from the Mount Rushmore site toward our location." She glanced up now, let her eyes skitter over John, toward Stella, then land on Allison. Licking her lips, she looked back down at the laptop. "There's one signal. One phone that I can identify for certain."

"Do you know whose phone it is?"

"No. He'd have to make a call for me to grab that information. Or text someone. I can't believe he hasn't done either."

"If it's Donovan Steele, you need to remember the man has an IQ of 132 which puts him solidly in the top 3% of the population. He would know enough to not make a phone call or send a text."

"Why is the device even on?" Stella asked.

"How else would he find us? The man isn't carrying around topographic maps for the entire country, and most people don't have a sextant."

"A what?" Jasmine asked.

He ignored her and kept his attention on Stella. She was the loose cannon here. "There's a reason that I gave our coordinates in decimal degrees. No matter how smart the man is, he'll need a cellular device to find us."

"And you're certain that he and Kate will walk into a trap, just the two of them, with no armed back-up ... for her?"

The derision in Stella's voice almost made John laugh. She never could understand the power of interpersonal relationships.

John decided it was best not to answer the question. He turned back to Jasmine. "Anything on Spencer?"

"No." Now Jasmine pulled in her bottom lip, making her look ridiculously like a pouting pre-teen.

"If he's alive, he'll be in contact through the back channels. Keep those open and monitor them closely."

Jasmine nodded. John gestured toward the front porch of the cabin, and Stella followed him, albeit with an eye roll.

"Is there a reason this cabin isn't properly stocked with supplies? I could use a drink, John. You know I operate better when I have a drink."

"Stella, I need you to focus. This operation is not going as planned."

"Why do you say that?"

He explained about the lack of news coverage.

"But the crowds were there, drawn to your idiotic monoliths. The bomb went off. The biohazard that you purchased at no small cost to the both of us was released."

"All true. But if no one was in the visitor's center at the time the weapon detonated, then the biohazard didn't spread. It's heavy. Remember? Heavy particles. We chose that because it was what was available, it has a high mortality rate, and we were fairly certain we could push the tourists into the confined area."

"Then what went wrong?"

"I don't know. I don't know that anything went wrong. Maybe they're keeping it out of the news, but it should at least be on social media."

"We gambled everything on this," Stella reminded him. Her voice was now calm, almost robotic. She'd somehow flipped a switch, turned off the madness for a moment, zeroed in on the mission. "Not just our accumulated resources, but also our future resources. We shorted every stock that Spencer's program said would suffer a dramatic decline after a national emergency. No emergency ... no stock decline ... no chance to make millions. Effectively, we'll be out of business."

She might be out of business.

The Anarchists for Tomorrow might be out of business.

John wouldn't. He'd had enough sense to put money in undisclosed offshore accounts.

"He's coming," Jasmine called.

John and Stella rushed back into the cabin and hovered near the laptop that Jasmine was staring at. A map grid showing their location filled the entire screen, and on the map grid, coming toward them at a steady clip, was a small red dot.

Donovan Steele.

Kate Jackson.

This operation might not produce the success he'd hoped for. America might still refuse to wake up to the abuses of their government and the enslavement of their lives by big tech, but he wouldn't walk away empty-handed. He would have his revenge. Even if it was simply killing the three people who had thwarted his plans for the last several years. Albert Pike, an American lawyer in the 1800s, had once said that "War is a series of catastrophes which result in victory." John liked to consider himself a student of history. And that quote, it applied to him, the AT, the entire plan. They had suffered catastrophes. Several had been at the hands of Quinn, Steele, and Jackson.

He wasn't insane like Stella; however, he understood the necessity to be done with those three.

The death of a few sacrificed for the needs of the many.

Yeah. He liked the sound of that.

Tell me again why I can't kill her...

Arthur Quinn ruined my life.

He stole from me.

I killed him.

I killed him.

I killed him.

The words played on an endless loop through Allison's mind. Had she heard the woman say those things? Or had she dreamt them? Was it even remotely possible that this elderly woman had killed her father?

Allison pushed her mind away from the past, away from that pivotal moment of her childhood, and back to the present. She could still make out the whining voice of the woman who had shot her. Stella Gonzalez. Kate had told her a lot about the financier of the AT, and still the shot had come as a complete surprise. The woman wasn't merely ruthless. She was unhinged.

Allison had wavered in and out of consciousness as John Howard and the young woman—what was her name.... Jasper, Janice, Jasmine. John and Jasmine had carried her down a trail. Not far. They'd stashed a car—not just any car, but the red Voltaris she and Kate had seen behind the Rusty Spur. In the darkness, the thing had looked other-worldly. High-tech. Expensive.

She'd passed out when John, who was driving, had maneuvered the vehicle from the trail to pavement. It had felt like the one time she'd ridden in a rally car, something that young agents-in-training had thought sounded like a reward. It hadn't been. When they'd reached 130 mph, her heightened adrenaline and the G-forces she was experiencing had done their work. She'd puked as soon as the car had slammed to a stop—puked on the ground, fortunately, as the driver hadn't looked like the understanding type.

The ride tonight had been eerily similar to that other ride, so many years ago.

Her mind wanted to stay back there, in the past, where nothing could hurt her. She wanted to ignore the agony that was her leg, but she needed to focus. Allison had been shot more than once, but this felt different. Her leg was one intense, throbbing pain the likes of which she'd never experienced before. Had the bullet shattered a bone? Grazed a nerve? Torn through muscle? Had it done all three? And how was she going to be of any use to Donovan and Kate when they arrived?

And they were coming.

Jasmine was jabbering on excitedly about a red dot.

Stella clapped her hands.

John's voice had changed from downtrodden dread to excited anticipation.

"What's our plan?" Stella asked. "And what are we going to do with her? You promised me I could..."

"I know what I promised. Let's just get through the next few minutes. The road they took into the canyon stops here." He leaned closer to the map on Jasmine's screen. "They'll have to walk to the exact coordinates, which I'm sure they will. You and Jasmine will greet them. I'll take up position here. Your job is to engage them in conversation. If they ask to see her, drag her outside for them. I don't care. Just keep them in position long enough for me to get off two shots."

"Why are you the one shooting? I'm good with a gun."

"Stella, do you want to walk through the forest to this position?" He tapped a spot on the screen. "Because that's where you need to be so that your bullets don't take out the good guys—us!"

"No. I don't want to do that, and I'll thank you not to take that tone with me."

"Um, guys. They've stopped. I think they're here."

All three leaned toward the screen.

"Let's do this," John said, picking up a rifle with a thermal scope.

"Do me a favor, John. Don't kill Kate. Just wing her. I'd like to take the final shot. I think I'm owed that, given she was such a traitor to the cause."

"Sure, Stella. I'll try to wing her."

"And I can kill Allison when this is done? Promise."

"Pinky swear. You can kill Allison when I get back." He retrieved the handgun from the band of his pants, stepped closer to Stella, and handed it to her. "Not until I give you the word."

And then he was gone, slipping into the night.

Stella walked back out onto the porch. Jasmine remained glued to her screen. Allison slowly and carefully allowed her eyes to open wider. She took in as much of the cabin as she could from her position on the bed. She didn't see any additional weapons. Surely, they had more weapons. John had left the handgun with Stella, which was puzzling. She was as likely to shoot him as shoot Allison. When screaming, Stella had seemed hysterical. Then seconds later she was calm, even detached. Allison had to remember she was not dealing with a rational person. This woman—Stella Gonzalez—would shoot first and talk about it later.

I killed him.

I killed him.

I killed him.

Adrenaline pumped through Allison's veins, and with it, the last of her grogginess slipped away. She considered that a good thing, as she could think more clearly. But it was also a bad thing, rendering the pain from her leg even more encompassing.

She could close her eyes, slip back into unconsciousness, let the dreams and the memories take her to a place where the pain was less.

She snapped her eyes open.

Had she passed out?

Jasmine was now standing at the cabin's door, and it sounded to Allison like they were out there waiting for someone to approach.

Allison gathered what little strength she had, committed to the only plan she could think of, and waited.

She didn't have to wait long.

Chapter Eighteen

Donovan and Kate waited, giving Grey time to get into position. The coordinates given to them lay dead ahead —dead north. Grey Hopkins, former U.S. Army sniper, team leader, and staff sergeant with a rank of E-6, thought whoever was laying this trap would set up to the east in case the operation dragged on. "He'll face west. Wouldn't want the sun in his eyes."

Kate couldn't resist countering with, "Or *she'll* face west to keep the sun out of *her* eyes."

"Absolutely." He didn't rush off. Just stood there in the darkness, in the starlight, holding the SR-25 that was equipped with the latest and most advanced thermal scope, waiting for Kate to ask her next question.

"What about you? The sun will be in your eyes."

"Sun won't rise until 5:18. Gives us almost ninety minutes. This will be over long before that."

His confidence was both comforting and alarming. Who was this guy? Sure, he had military experience, but did that naturally transfer to taking down terrorists in Spearfish Canyon? And how had he ended up with the National Park Service? Kate had questions, but Donovan and Allison both trusted him. That would have to be enough for her.

They gave him fifteen minutes to move into position.

Would John Howard have Allison hog-tied in a clearing? She couldn't be stuffed into the boot of a car or cuffed in a backseat. There was no road that she'd seen. Not beyond this point. Not on their SAT phone's GPS. Apparently, the only way to 44.338140, -103.964640 was to push through the dense foliage.

Donovan nudged her shoulder with his, and she gave him a thumbs-up. Time to finish this. She wanted it to be over—the years she'd spent undercover, the lives John Howard had stolen and ruined, the arrogance and ruthlessness of the AT. She wanted to cut off the beast's head once and for all.

They made their way through the heavy undergrowth. Kate could hear the splash of waterfalls in the distance, to the southwest maybe. The air was filled with the smell of pine trees. The coolness of the pre-dawn air surprised her. She had the sense of the canyon walls rising on both sides, but in the darkness, she couldn't guess how far up they went. Everything about this hike through the woods felt like walking through a dream, through her worst nightmare, along a path fraught with danger and monsters and an evil that was difficult to conceive.

Nightmarish for sure, but in another way she was more awake, more alert than she'd ever been in her entire life. Kate felt as if she were walking toward her destiny, toward some pivotal moment in her life.

Donovan had punched the coordinates into his SAT phone. Now he stopped her with a hand and held the screen out to her. One hundred yards ahead—the length of a football field. She'd watched countless games with her brothers, with her friends.

Allison was there, just one hundred yards away.

They crept forward slowly until she could just make out a cabin, dim lantern light, and Stella Gonzalez standing on the porch.

"Might as well come on into the clearing. Certainly, you don't think we brought you here just to shoot you."

There was little doubt that was exactly what they'd done.

Donovan stepped closer to the clearing, though he remained in the shadows. "Where is she?"

"Allison? She's in the cabin, of course. We won't renege on our deal."

"We don't have a deal."

"Ah, yes. Well, what we need is information. Provide us that, and we'll release her."

"Information on what?"

"The JCTF, of course."

Kate wasn't buying it, and she knew Donovan wasn't either. Stella was stalling for time, but why?

"We need to see her."

"And I need to see Kate. After all, this was always a two- for-one deal."

Kate stepped next to Donovan. She wondered how well Stella could see them. Maybe she could make out two shadows in the predawn darkness. Was that enough?

"First, show us Allison," Donovan said.

Stella sighed dramatically, as if extremely irritated by the request. And yet, she didn't argue.

"Give me a minute. She's having some trouble walking."

Kate felt, more than saw, Donovan stiffen. They both had known Allison was injured. They'd heard the gunshot on the video, seen Allison fall to the ground, watched Stella drug her. Knowing it or watching it on a video was one thing. Waiting to see it in person was another.

Unexplainably, two spotlights positioned near the door of the cabin and facing the clearing blinked on, effectively blinding Donovan and Kate and causing the occupants that stepped out on the porch to appear as silhouettes.

And still, even given the visual obstacles, Kate recognized Jasmine as soon as she moved through the door. John Howard had set off on the biggest terrorist attack of his career with Stella, Spencer, and Jasmine? Was that by choice or because of the raid on their facilities in Wyoming? She didn't have long to think about it because Donovan had moved forward. She reached out and pulled him back.

Allison stood, or was being carried, between Stella and Jasmine. Stella was having trouble with her half of Allison's weight, which clearly did not top 135. But Stella was old and not particularly fit. In fact, she was usually drinking heavily. The shaking in her hands told Kate that she'd been missing the hourly scotch splashed over ice she'd grown so found of.

"Here she is. Everything's right as rain, or will be as soon as you get her to a hospital. You might not want to dally. She's lost a fair amount of blood."

"What information do you want?" Donovan's voice was cold, calculating, all business.

"Size of the task force at Mount Rushmore, number of people working the national issues, and most importantly—where you aren't looking. A girl needs a place to lie low and wait for things to calm down. I'm going to need you to step farther out into the clearing, though. My hearing isn't what it used to be."

Which sounded fishy, even to Kate, who was processing several critical things at once. Allison's injury in her leg. The spotlights. Jasmine's cowering posture. Stella.

The spotlights.

The spotlights.

The spotlights were there to—

Four things happened at the same moment.

Stella stuck her right hand into her pocket, no doubt in an attempt to hide the tremors in her hand. Allison raised her head, shouted, "Get down," and fell into Stella, who toppled over. Jasmine screamed and hit the porch floor as if she'd been slugged. Kate heard the sonic crack of an SR-25 as Donovan threw himself on top of her, knocking her to the ground.

Did she hear the thwack of the bullet finding its mark?

Could she smell hot metal and gunpowder?

Birds cried and flew from the surrounding trees. A coyote howled. Someone was weeping.

And then, as suddenly as it started, everything stopped.

The woods, once again, fell silent.

John Howard had set up the shot perfectly. He only needed Donovan and Kate to take a few steps into the clearing. He wanted a kill shot. No use wounding them. He did not plan on "winging" Kate. This was his chance to end his enemy. Once done, he'd go back to the cabin and kill Allison, Stella, and Jasmine.

He'd make a clean break.

He'd start over.

As he waited for the spotlights to come on, he thought of his wife and daughter. It had been so long now that he sometimes had trouble remembering their faces, the sound of their voices, the way it felt to go home to a family. He didn't dwell on those missing parts of his life because he was a forward-looking man. Science didn't currently provide a way to bring the two most deserving people in the world back from the dead, so he had to be satisfied with making the world a better place.

A safer place.

A place where a foreign assassin wasn't able to sneak into a country and take out a CIA operative's family. A place where one's government did not allow such things to happen. The explosion of technology, and the nation's dependence on it, had only made things exponentially worse.

"We'll be together soon, John."

John knew he couldn't focus on his wife's voice, not now. He needed to be completely focused.

"I love you, daddy."

A tear slipped down his cheek, but he didn't brush it away.

He didn't move at all. John Howard kept his eyes on the cabin, the front porch, the space in front of the cabin. He knew that he could make the two shots. It felt ... preordained.

He heard the sonic crack of a long-range rifle, had a split second to realize he hadn't yet pressed the trigger, and then everything went—

Allison didn't pass out when she hit the ground on top of Stella. Pain seared through her leg. Pain so all-encompassing that for a moment she wondered if it was worth struggling against. She understood that she'd done even more damage to her leg. She'd seen Stella going for the gun and known that was the moment that she needed to act.

She needed to save Donovan and Kate.

The pain rolled over her like a wave.

Time slipped.

She woke with her head cradled in Donovan's lap. His hands gently framing her face. He bent close. Whispered. "We're here. It's going to be okay. We're here, Alli. It's over."

She didn't forget the pain, but she pushed it away long enough to realize she had passed out for the space of a few heartbeats. Passed out and come to in the arms of the man she loved. That would make a wonderful scene in a romance novel.

Donovan was now barking into a SAT phone. Calling for a medevac. Calling for JCTF back-up. Giving their location in digital degree coordinates. Telling them to hurry.

She heard Kate hissing, "Move, Stella. Please make a move for it. Give me a reason to shoot you where you stand."

She heard Jasmine sobbing. Why was Jasmine sobbing?

Then there was another man's voice, saying he'd killed John Howard, saying it was over.

Kate sat on the steps leading to the cabin. The sun had risen over Spearfish Canyon. The place was as beautiful as she'd imagined. Towering canyon walls. Lush foliage. Summer wildflowers. The musical sound of water crashing over nearby falls.

Grey sat next to her.

The helicopter carrying Allison and Donovan was now a dot in the sky.

A crew from JCFT was processing the cabin, the woods, the vehicle stowed a few hundred yards away. John Howard's body had not yet been removed, but Stella and Jasmine had been placed in a government vehicle and whisked away. She wondered about their last vision of the great outdoors being a place so beautiful. They didn't deserve that, but the fact that they'd be spending the rest of their lives in prison eased the bitterness of the thought.

"Wow," Grey said.

"Yeah."

"Is it always like this? Your job?"

"Not always..." She pulled the last word out like taffy, because it had been like that for almost as long as she could remember. The years undercover, the flight from Middle Earth, teaming up with Allison, months spent calculating where the AT would strike next, the long drive to South Dakota. Crazy Horse. Mount Rushmore.

"She's going to be okay," he said.

"I think so. I hope so."

"Donovan's over the moon about Allison."

"It hasn't always been that way."

"No?"

Allison had told Kate about the Grand Canyon op, about all that had gone wrong and the few things that had gone right, about Donovan and his team finally arriving after Allison had killed four people. About the guilt Allison carried that she should have called for back-up, should have called Donovan sooner than she had. About her resentment and her fear that she was losing herself in this compulsion to avenge her father's murder.

"Let's just say they worked together for some time before they realized, or admitted, they cared for each other."

"And Allison's father was murdered?"

"That's a long story."

Grey looked at her, held her gaze, smiled slightly. How long had it been since a man smiled at her that way? How long had it been since she'd let herself breathe in and out without wondering if it was her last breath?

"Maybe not long exactly, but it's complicated." She finger-combed her hair, wondered what she must look like.

Grey laughed, brushed a few leaves and dirt off her shoulder, left his hand there a fraction of a second. "I'd love to hear it."

"Hungry?"

"I am actually."

"Let's catch a ride on the next chopper. Find a place to eat. I'll tell you about Allison and Donovan's history, and about her dad. You can tell me what it's like to be a park ranger."

"Deal."

They both stood and stepped out into the clearing. Kate paused, closed her eyes, lifted her face to the sky. They'd survived, and they'd taken down thc AT. They'd killed John Howard. Arrested Stella and Jasmine. There were still some minions out there. It wasn't a perfect conclusion to a very terrible time in her life. But for the moment, it was good enough.

Chapter Nineteen

Allison and Donovan sat under an old oak tree at the top of the hill. The beauty of October in the Texas Hill Country wasn't lost on either of them. The leaves on the elm trees had turned golden. The live oaks had dropped their acorns. The pecan trees made her think of giant sentinels.

She liked that idea.

Trees guarding the ranch.

Angels surrounding what felt to her like holy ground.

"You're awfully quiet over there."

"Yeah?"

"Leg okay?"

"Leg is fine." Which was almost true. Two surgeries. One month of rehab followed by three months of outpatient therapy. The doctors had been honest—told her she might not be running marathons in the future, but she could return to duty one day. Maybe in six months. Her goal was five.

"I had a dream last night," she said.

"Yeah?"

They were sitting side by side on a rise of the property, backs resting against the giant live oak that was certainly over a hundred years old. Maybe two hundred. Maybe three. Allison had suggested having an arborist out to estimate the age. Polly had laughed at that. "Honey, it'll provide the same amount of shade whether we know the age or not." Which had been followed by a kiss on top of her head. Something that always made Allison feel like a child. And cherished.

"Are you going to tell me about it?"

Donovan had been with her throughout the entire rehab. He'd insisted on taking leave. Even rented a car that she could get in and out of easier than his precious Corvette. He'd been her rock as much as Polly and Kate and Grey and Edward and this ranch had.

"It was about my dad. We were back there, back under the redwoods." She looked up, looked through the live oak's limbs to the impossibly blue sky beyond.

Donovan didn't push. Didn't ask. He reached for her hand.

"I was a kid again. Wearing my Dora Explorer shirt. My back pressed against that tree. But this time, my dad came for me. He reached for my hand. Took it in his..." She glanced down at her hand in Donovan's. What was it about two hands, clasped together, that said so much about two people?

She closed her eyes, tried to recapture the essence of the dream. "There was no shot. No bang or fear or trembling all night. He just reached for my hand, and then we walked away, walked down this trail that was absolutely beautiful."

"Yeah?" Donovan ran his thumb over hers.

"Yeah." She stood without help, something she couldn't have done two months ago. Reached for this man who had been by her side for so long, through so much, that she couldn't imagine breathing without him.

He grinned.

Let her pretend she was pulling him to his feet.

"I'd like to take you there," she said.

"To the redwoods?"

"Yup."

"I still have some time I can take. Let's do it."

Things were that simple for Donovan.

Let's do it.

"Okay. Let's."

They heard tires across gravel, saw Edward's old truck making its way through the gate and up the caliche road. Polly and Kate stepped out onto the porch. Kate leaned toward Polly, seemed to say something, and Polly gestured toward the old truck.

Kate gave her a hug, then hurried to meet the truck.

When Grey Hopkins stepped out, she threw herself in his arms.

"Those two fell for each other awfully quick."

"All those hours sitting by your bedside, sharing terrible vending machine coffee—"

"Pushing me through rehab."

"Hey. We all did that."

Allison put her arm through his, leaned into him for the familiarity and comfort of his body next to hers more than because she needed the help. They walked toward the ranch, toward their friends and her family and their future.

Allison felt immeasurably lighter. She'd released her burden of guilt, of being the one to survive, of wondering what she—a child—could have done differently, of wondering what she—an agent—would need to do to resolve, finally, the terrible tragedy of her life.

It had been resolved—a little.

And she'd also accepted that every life had its tragedies. She'd learn to live with hers, but she'd also set down that guilt. She glanced over her shoulder, back at the live oak. Yup. Probably three hundred years old. She'd put money on it. That live oak had witnessed untold broken hearts, heard the lament of countless tragedies, seen the four seasons come and go. Seen the people come and go.

The tree remained.

Their love for one another remained.

Allison's love for her father, and his for her, would always remain. And the fact that she was finally stepping forward, accepting the love of Donovan and Polly, Edward, Kate and Grey ... that was okay. That was what her father would want.

"Want to go next week?" she asked.

"To northern California?"

"Yup."

"Think you're up to riding in the Corvette?"

Her laughter rang out, followed them down to the ranch house, to dinner around an old oak table, and the fellowship of people she loved.

It was everything she'd ever hoped for—and more.

So much more.

The End

Enjoy **FREE** bonus scenes and novels when you join my mailing list. Plus, get updates on new releases, deals, and more from Vannetta Chapman. Click below to sign up.

CLICK HERE TO SIGN UP

Not sure if you're a subscriber? Provide your email again. We'll check and send you a link to your free book. You will also continue to receive exclusive offers in your inbox.

Thank you for reading, ***Oath of Allegiance.*** I hope you enjoyed the story. If you did, please consider rating the book or leaving a review at Amazon, Bookbub, or Goodreads.

Keep reading for a preview of *Veil of Mystery*, the prequel to my Kessler Effect series.

Author's Note

While much of the technology described in this book has appeared frequently in news reports and major motion pictures, part of it is only rumored to be possible. For example, Starlink phones are only rumored to exist. There is also no evidence of a weaponized form of Marburg, as described in this book.

In September 2024, communication devices, including pagers and walkie-talkies used by the armed group Hezbollah, exploded across Lebanon. According to various news sources, these devices received a message and seconds later, they exploded. Thirty-two people were killed and thousands were injured. Although, according to multiple sources, this technology does not currently exist, it is widely believed that Israel was behind the attacks. It is thought that an explosive compound had been hidden within the devices, and then a message was sent, which triggered the explosion. This is not the first such high-tech warfare in the region. In 2020, Israel used an AI-assisted robot, controlled by a remote satellite, to kill one of Iran's top nuclear scientists.

The Voltaris X does not exist; however, I based its capabilities on the Rimac Nevera, the Waymo Autonomous Vehicle, and the Lucid Air Dream. As for the tunnel beneath John Howard's lair, I referred to specifications of Elon Musk's prospective tunnel from San Marcos, Texas to Austin, Texas.

Mysterious monoliths have appeared in Utah, California, Romania, Poland, Wales, and Las Vegas, to name a few. Some were removed by local authorities, others by individuals. Some disappeared as inexplicably as they appeared.

In 1868, the Treaty of Fort Laramie granted the Black Hills to the Sioux Nation. Following the discovery of gold, the U.S. government seized the land in 1877. Very little of the Black Hills is currently designated as tribal land; however, some tribal organizations have purchased small parcels of land in the area in recent years. To further the plot of this novel, I have included characters of both the Sioux Nation and the Crow Creek Sioux Tribe. My characters are fictional and any mistakes I've made in representation are solely my own. Likewise, while there is a descendent of the Ziolkowski currently working on the senior executive team, the person in my story is fictional.

An Excerpt From

Veil of Mystery
A Kessler Effect Prequel

June 6, 20~~
Alpine, Texas

The first anomaly occurred on Tuesday morning at fourteen minutes after ten. Keme Lopez noted the time, confirmed that his back-up system had taken a screenshot of all open windows, and replayed the video that had appeared on Twitter. There wasn't much to it—a mere fourteen seconds from start to finish. Already it was at the top of his Twitter feed.

He sat back, trying to understand what he'd seen. Trying to come up with a better explanation than the Twitter universe had. Slowly, cautiously—as if playing the video might cause some danger to befall him and his family—he again clicked *play*.

A woman with short blonde hair sobbed as she recorded live. He could see the *Recording Live* button at the bottom of the screen. The video definitely represented something that had happened in real time. From the looks of the people in the background, what he was seeing had actually occurred.

As tears streamed down her face and in words that were nearly incoherent, she told her husband that she loved him.

Keme paused the video.

He zoomed in on passengers in the background. Some huddled together, heads bowed, praying. A mother in the next row rocked her child back and forth. Many passengers had their hands over their faces, and about a third sat in the classic "prepare for crash" position. Several men stood, though the nose-down angle of the plane obviously made that difficult. They seemed to be looking out the window.

When Keme zoomed in more, he was able to see clear blue skies. So this plane crash—if that's what it was—was not weather-related.

Mechanical failure? But there was no smoke that he could see. No holes in the plane. It seemed to be simply falling from the sky.

A soft rap on his open door jerked him back to the present—a June morning in Alpine, Texas.

"I'm headed outside to work in the garden," Lucy said.

Keme's wife was a professor of literature at Sul Ross University. She was five foot, four inches with a curvy figure and brown hair—the tips dyed with turquoise streaks. Keme had married up, and he realized that anew every single day.

"What would make a plane fall from the sky?"

"Excuse me?"

"Mechanical failure, a bomb exploding, maybe a pilot who had a heart attack..."

"Not the last one." She moved into the room and stared at his screen, then reached past him and clicked *Play*. She watched the video in silence, then played it again. Finally, she stepped back, leaning against the doorframe and staring up at the ceiling.

He waited.

Finally her brown eyes met his.

"That's awful. Is it real?"

"Seems to be. Why did you say '*not the last one*?'"

"Because that's what a co-pilot rides along for, and I think...I think a plane switches to automatic pilot if something unusual happens."

"Probably so."

"When was that video recorded?"

Keme glanced at the time on his computer. "Almost fifteen minutes ago."

"Anything on the news sites?"

He clicked to a different tab and unmuted the window.

"The video was apparently taken aboard a direct flight from London to Austin just a few minutes ago. According to the FAA—"

The screen abruptly went to a plain blue background with *Please Stand By* displayed in a large font. Beneath it was a banner which read *We are experiencing technical problems at this time.*

"What happened?"

"I don't know." He again noted the time—10:30. "They've just stopped streaming."

He clicked over to two other news stations, but they both displayed the same blue screen with the same disclaimer.

"Is the internet down?"

"Doesn't seem to be." He clicked back to Twitter.

Top story—#Planecrash
Second story--#newsoutage

"An EMP?" Lucy crossed her arms, frowning at the screen.

"The internet is still up. I guess it could be a localized EMP, but the odds that it would affect all news outlets seems... impossible."

Lucy squeezed his shoulder, then kissed his cheek. "Let me know if anything else bizarre happens."

"Where are you going?"

"To weed the garden."

Which was exactly like Lucy. She was somewhat unflappable. A nuclear bomb could be headed their way, and she'd say, "I certainly can't stop a nuke. Might as well weed the garden." She was very big on ignoring things out of her scope of influence. Maybe not ignoring, but she certainly didn't spend hours worrying over it. He envied her that, even as he watched her walk away.

His eyes scanned the shelves in his office which held a wide variety of items that he thought of as simply—*my history*. There were water sticks, deer antlers, arrow heads, and rocks. The collection represented his Native American heritage. His mother was one quarter Kiowa. His father was Hispanic, and it was from his father that he'd inherited his handiness. For his Pop that meant farm equipment. For Keme, it meant computers.

A long workspace counter stretched along two walls of his office, and it was filled with computers. At the age of forty-two, he managed to make a pretty good living fixing people's computers. Alpine was only six thousand folks. Given their remote location in the southwest corner of Texas, computers were how they remained connected to the rest of the world.

He turned his attention back to his monitor.

For the next twenty minutes he browsed the world wide web, but there was no consensus as to what had happened. Definitely no official statement.

Then he clicked back to Twitter and saw that the plane crash had been bumped down to the number two spot. In its place was the hashtag #stockmarketcollapse.

Keme no longer invested his money in the stock market, but he did stay apprised of the general situation. There'd been a lot of "collapses" in the last few years. It usually meant the market dropped ten percent then rebounded twelve to fifteen percent the next day. He was pretty sure the market was manipulated so that the ups and downs made the rich richer and kept everyone not in that group out.

Just another of your conspiracy theories, Lucy was fond of saying.

He clicked on #stockmarketcollapse and scanned through the posts.

As he watched, the ticker went from a seventy-five percent loss to an eighty percent loss.

The DOW had dropped eighty percent? That wasn't possible. Circuit breaker rules had been put in place in 1988 to protect companies against panic selling. He tried clicking over to another site, but now his machine seemed frozen. None of the sites would refresh. He leaned back in his chair to check his modem. Red lights blinked back at him.

It wasn't unusual for the internet to go down in Alpine. They were, after all, in a rural part of Texas. Keme picked up his cellphone and stared at the icon in the upper right. No internet signal at all. Furthermore, when he tried to place a call, it wouldn't connect.

So the internet was down, as well as the cell towers?

Pocketing the device, he grabbed his hat and stepped outside.

Lucy was squatting in front of the tomato plants. Sitting back on her heels, she asked, "Any answers?"

"Nope."

"More questions?"

"Yup. Internet is out completely and so are the phones."

"Huh."

Keme glanced north toward Alpine. "The stock market crashed just before the internet went down."

"By how much?"

"Eighty percent."

Lucy wiped away sweat from her brow. "I didn't think that was possible."

"It shouldn't be."

She stood and brushed at the dirt on the back of her jeans. Walking over to him, she cocked her head and studied him. "You're worried."

He shrugged, then admitted, "Yeah."

"Akule is fine, honey. She's right there..." Lucy jerked a thumb toward Alpine. "We can go check on her if you like."

Their daughter had recently moved back to Alpine, but their son, Paco, lived with his wife and children in the Dallas area. If something big was happening, Keme would like to have his family close.

"Have you called Tanda?"

He smiled, kissed her forehead, and pulled her into his arms. "Phones are out. Remember?"

"Oh, yeah." She snuggled against him. "Sounds like you won't be fixing anyone's computer this morning. How about you and I go inside and—"

At that moment there was an explosion that caused the ground to tremble.

"What—"

"Look."

A cloud of smoke was rising on the horizon. Something had exploded. The scream of emergency vehicles immediately followed. Whatever was happening, it was happening in the middle of Alpine.

Veil of Mystery is a 51 page prequel, available as a **free** download with all ebook retailers.

Also by Vannetta Chapman

DEFENDING AMERICA SERIES

Coyote's Revenge (Book 1)

Roswell's Secret (Book 2)

KESSLER EFFECT SERIES

Veil of Mystery (Book 1, Prequel)

Veil of Anarchy (Book 2, Novel)

Veil of Confusion (Book 3, Novel)

Veil of Destruction (Book 4, Novel)

Veil of Stillness (Book 5, Novel)

Veil of Hope (Book 6, Novel)

ALLISON QUINN SERIES

Her Solemn Oath (Book 1, Prequel)

Support and Defend (Book 2, Novel)

Against All Enemies (Book 3, Novel)

Oath of Allegiance (Book 4, Novel)

FOR A COMPLETE LIST OF MY BOOKS, VISIT MY

Complete Book List